CW00762492

De a..y Cruise

DAWN BROOKES

Large Print

A Rachel Prince Mystery

DAWN BROOKES

OAKWOOD PUBLISHING

This novel is entirely a work of fiction. The names, characters and incidents portrayed are the work of the author's imagination. Any resemblance to actual persons, living or dead is entirely coincidental except for those in the public domain. Although real life places are depicted in settings, all situations and people related to those places are fictional.

www.dawnbrookespublishing.com
Large Print Edition 2018
Large Print ISBN: 978-1-9998575-7-8
Copyright © DAWN BROOKES 2018

DAWN BROOKES asserts the moral right to be identified as the author of this Work. All rights reserved in all media.

Cover Design by Janet Dado

To Ruth

Friends make life more fun

Chapter 1

At three o'clock on a damp, drizzly morning, a man's bulky body could be seen floating face-downward in the Moskva River, should anyone crossing the Krymsky Bridge in Moscow peer below. The killer had spent days meticulously surveying the area, choosing time and place carefully to prevent that from happening.

By the time the lifeless body was found it should have been carried further south of where the killer now stood admiring his callous handiwork. Satisfied he'd completed the grisly task, he walked a few miles back to the lively bar that would serve as his alibi should he need one. He'd already made certain of being seen by several different people before slipping away. On his return, he'd get himself noticed again to give the impression he'd never left.

After slipping in to the bar unnoticed, he ordered a double vodka and bought the barman a drink before settling in a corner booth. Another man joined him and he handed over a thick envelope containing one thousand US dollars. Payment for the intelligence he'd received. Good information as it turned out.

Later that morning he awoke with a hangover. After packing a suitcase, he travelled by taxi to Sheremetyevo airport, but not before scanning the local radio channels in his apartment. Reports of the body of a Moscow businessman found in the river at dawn sounded low key. Initial police statements suggested the authorities were treating the death as suicide.

Perfect, just what the heartless killer had hoped. Everything was going to plan.

"One down, one to go," he muttered before getting into his taxi.

Being booked on an afternoon flight to London, he called his sister and arranged to meet at the Ritz for dinner, explaining he planned to leave for Southampton the next day.

Once on board the plane, he reclined his seat and took a nap, pleased to be in the quiet of business class. It had been a busy three days.

Chapter 2

"It's not a great idea, letting you loose on another cruise after last year. You know I'm worried, don't you?"

The handsome Carlos hauled Rachel's suitcase from the boot of his 1970s Ford Capri. Rachel gazed into his sensitive dark brown eyes and laughed, remembering her first cruise – complete with a murderer on board.

"This one will be indulgent luxury, I'm confident."

"Well in that case, my lady, here we are at your first port of call." Carlos had driven up from London to Leeds, where Rachel had worked the night before, and brought her down to her parents' home in Hertfordshire this afternoon.

"Hm, in spite of a minor hiccup."

Carlos kept the Capri in immaculate condition, it being his pride and joy, but it remained prone to minor mechanical problems and he'd had to change the fan belt before they'd left as it was slipping. Feigning hurt, he took her hand.

Rachel's parents stood on the doorstep, unable to contain their excitement. Rachel rushed forward to hug her mother while her father helped Carlos unpack the rest of the car and shook his hand.

"Good to meet you again, Carlos. Will you be staying for dinner?"

Carlos looked unsure, still a little intimidated by Rachel's father, the Reverend Brendan Prince.

"Oh, do stay," Rachel cajoled, knowing how he felt, but eager for him to get to know her parents, whom she loved dearly.

Carlos coughed, nervously. "How can I refuse such a kind invitation? Thank you, I will."

The men carried the suitcase and bags indoors while Rachel and her mum walked through to the kitchen.

"He's afraid dad can't talk about anything but religion." Rachel laughed. "I've tried to explain that he's most eloquent and can converse about many things, but Carlos can't seem to get past it."

"And your dad doesn't get past how Robert treated you, breaking your heart and calling off the engagement. It makes it tough for him to accept another man in your life just yet. When he's overprotective, it makes him less easy going than usual."

"Oh, Mum. What are we to do with them? Carlos is not at all like Robert and Dad needn't worry, I won't be rushing into a serious relationship for a long time."

Her mother looked concerned at this revelation, but didn't press.

"They'll become used to each other. Your father's a reasonable man, and when he relaxes, Carlos might find him more approachable. He'll talk all day about cars!" Mrs Prince turned towards a pot of freshly percolated coffee.

"It's wonderful to see you, Mum."

"It's great to see you too, Rachel, we miss you. Your father and I worry about you taking another cruise, though, after what happened last year."

"Now you're sounding like Carlos. I'm positive that was a one-off." Rachel laughed again. "Sarah will be there, and I need a break, Mum."

Rachel wondered what her mother would think if she knew all she'd been going through and how much she needed a respite from policing. While her mother busied herself making drinks and preparing dinner, Rachel excused herself and took her coffee outside to the garden. Carlos and her father had disappeared; she assumed this was a positive thing, but hoped Carlos wasn't being given a pep talk.

Rachel lingered outside, sitting on a swing seat on the large paved patio and surveying the grounds where she had grown up. The vicarage stood tall, an imposing Victorian building with eight bedrooms and ample space upstairs and down. Generous sized gardens displayed an ancient oak, large acacia trees, an apple orchard and a multitude of shrubs lining the borders that shielded the vicarage from the church, next door. Rachel inhaled the refreshing smell of recently mown grass. Her father found gardening a therapeutic hobby; his garden was his haven where he went to unwind.

He took his job seriously and spent a lot of time visiting parishioners; hence, his church bucked the national trend of diminishing numbers. It was a two-edged sword, though, because it led to her father being permanently on call. Rachel's mum also kept busy by proxy, entertaining or supporting various causes and village activities, although the Parish Council had recently agreed to employ a youth worker to take up the slack.

Rachel took a sip of coffee, recalling the events of the last six months. It had begun one Monday evening when she and her colleague, Tim Bryson, responded to an emergency call. The street they were directed to was on a housing estate renowned for violence. They heard a commotion as soon as Tim parked the squad car, getting as close as he could to the noise, but the sounds were coming from behind a building with narrow access.

They hurried towards the noise and Tim gave chase to someone. He hadn't seen the other person in Rachel's line of sight, visible in the shimmering moonlight, and she froze as the glistening metal of a knife caught her eye. Running towards the second man, she realised it was too late to save the teenager he'd stabbed straight through the heart in merciless fashion.

Shocked, she reached for her radio as the man lunged forwards, still wielding the bloodied knife. It caught her stab vest rather than her neck; she fell and her attacker raised his knife again.

Rachel had managed to loosen the telescopic truncheon she carried while going for her radio with the other hand, and she wielded it with enough power to knock the man off balance. As soon as he was down, she got to her feet and hit him anew as he sought to stab her from the ground. This time, he quietened down, so she could drag his hands behind his back and apply handcuffs.

She rushed over to the boy lying in a pool of blood and called for an ambulance and backup, but the boy was already dead. Rachel tried for what seemed like an eternity to resuscitate him before the ambulance arrived.

Tim came back. "Where the hell were you?" he shouted, but stopped as he registered the scene in front of him. Sirens and police appeared from everywhere. The ambulance arrived and paramedics took over from Rachel, confirming her fears that the boy was dead. The perpetrator was still on the ground, yelling abuse at anyone who would listen. "Police brutality, that's what this is. That deranged woman hit me without provocation. I was just passing by, trying to help, when the *filth* came at me like a howling banshee."

There had to be an internal investigation, despite it being obvious the man was lying. Rachel's nerves were shot for several months as the court case seemed to drag on forever. After she had given evidence, alongside DNA found on the knife and in the boy's wounds, and separate evidence found at the scene, it was enough for a guilty verdict to be returned, convicting the man of murder. Rachel felt relieved the trial was over, even though the image of that young boy, attacked for his mobile phone, would stay with her forever.

Reaching for the lukewarm coffee, she realised Carlos was sitting next to her, sidling closer.

"How long have you been here?"

"Long enough – still getting flashbacks?"

"Yep, but less vivid than before. I'll be better once I've had a holiday. At least the court case is over and I can get on with my life. Did I tell you they've nominated me for a bravery award?"

Rachel didn't tell Carlos that the perpetrator, Steven Tansley, had vowed to get revenge. The police had never caught his accomplice, but she suspected Tansley was more mouth than action. Despite a history of violence dating back to his teenage years, he didn't appear to have the kind of influence that would put her in danger. Nevertheless, it would pay to remain alert.

"Yes, sweetheart, you did and you deserve it." Carlos held her hand for a while and they sat in comfortable silence. The silence was broken when they heard excited shrieking coming from the house. Rachel turned and saw Sarah, her best friend, running towards her.

"Rachel, I've missed you. I couldn't wait until tomorrow so your parents invited me over to dinner."

Rachel hugged her friend. "That's great! You look really well." Sarah had a healthy glow and exuded happiness. She worked as a nurse on the cruise ship Rachel would join the next day, and had shared in the adventures of the previous year when a hitman had been on board.

"Hello, Carlos, it's wonderful to see you too." Sarah gave him a warm embrace, and then turned back to Rachel. "I have enjoyed three months off after completing my first nine-month contract on Queen Cruises so I should look well."

"Dinner's ready." Rachel's mum appeared at the French doors leading out to the patio. The excited trio followed her back into the house and enjoyed a very pleasant home-cooked coq au vin. Rachel's mum, a superb hostess and accomplished cook, never failed to deliver.

Rachel and Sarah nattered away over dinner as if they had never been apart. The girls had been friends since school days and Sarah's parents were good friends with the Princes, attending the church where Rachel's father was vicar. There were a few nervous glances shared between Rachel's parents and Carlos over dinner, but while Rachel knew they worried about her going on a cruise, at least their joint concern brought the men closer together.

"Thank you for dinner, Mrs Prince, Mr Prince, but I must head back to London now," Carlos announced once they had enjoyed an after-dinner coffee. Rachel knew he was working on a difficult case, although he seemed unable to discuss too many details. As a private investigator, he worked on many mundane cases, but this latest one was more complex. Rachel was worried he might be in danger, but accepted the danger that came with both of their jobs and knew they would have to learn to live with it.

Rachel and Carlos had been attracted to each other almost immediately after meeting the year before and had been dating ever since. Neither of them was in any rush to settle down. Agreeing to allow the relationship to blossom into what was now a healthy romance, they had recently discussed the possibilities of Rachel moving jobs to London as they didn't see enough of each other, but Rachel was cautious following her broken engagement. She sometimes wondered whether she could ever give her heart to another man after the pain of Robert's betrayal. Carlos told her he would wait for as long as it took, confiding in her that he too was afraid of long-term commitment.

Rachel accompanied him to the car, and he held her tight.

"Be careful, my darling. Stay away from danger."

"The only danger on this cruise will be that I might gain weight." She kissed him on the lips.

"Call me tomorrow and when you are in New York."

"I will. Carlos, please be careful yourself, won't you?"

"Don't worry, I'll be fine. I'll collect you from the port in two weeks. Ciao."

Carlos climbed into his beloved car and drove away. Rachel remained outside, watching until his car disappeared from view in the evening sunset before returning to the house.

Day 0

Chapter 3

The next morning, Rachel woke before dawn with bright sunlight penetrating the light curtains in her childhood bedroom. Looking out at the Hertfordshire countryside, Rachel brimmed with excitement. The sun was already burning away the remaining early morning mist.

Rachel was taking this break courtesy of Queen Cruises' generous offer of a free luxury cruise anywhere in the world. New York was a place she had always longed to visit – 'the city that never sleeps' had an exciting ring to it, and shopping was her top priority. The cruise had been booked months ago with Rachel hoping the court case would be over. Now, with Sarah's new contract starting, the timing couldn't have been better.

When Rachel arrived downstairs, her father was already up and dressed, and most of her luggage had miraculously loaded itself into the boot of his car. Rachel gave an exasperated sigh. He preferred to start early and had limited tolerance of tardiness. She should have known he'd be worried about traffic congestion and potential delays, so inevitably would want to leave extra time for the journey to Southampton.

"Dad, we don't need to leave for another hour," whined Rachel in a fruitless attempt to slow him down.

She texted Sarah to let her know they would be with her soon. The phone vibrated almost immediately; she looked at the screen.

"*I knew your dad would want to leave sharpish. I'm up and ready.*" Sarah's response was more patient than Rachel's. There was hardly any chance to say goodbye to her mother before she was bustled into the car.

"Enjoy yourself in New York, darling, and stay out of trouble." Her mother gave her a quick hug, rolling her eyes and turning to her husband. "Drive carefully, Brendan, there's plenty of time." She kissed him on the cheek.

Before long, they'd collected Sarah and nine-months' worth of baggage essentials for her second stint aboard the *Coral Queen*. They had sailed on the same ship the previous year. The drive to Southampton was uneventful; even the M25 motorway was relatively clear, a rarity. The girls discussed how they could meet up in between Sarah's shifts.

"I hope you'll manage with all the sea days on this cruise." Sarah had previously broached this with Rachel, but she was prepared, knowing there were six sea days each way with only two days in New York.

"Don't worry, I've brought a truckload of books and intend to chill and de-stress. I'll make full use of the luxurious suite your company has thrown in. I didn't get to experience the benefits first time round!"

Sarah smiled. "You've got that right. During the last trip I did to New York, though, we had rough weather mid Atlantic. The medical team hardly came up for air."

"Is Dr Bentley on this cruise?" Rachel had become acquainted with members of the medical team last year and she liked the chief medical officer.

"Yes, Graham's still working on board, and Alex has stayed on as baby doc, so things are fairly stable now."

Rachel grinned at the term *baby doc*, a label used for junior doctors working on board cruise ships. She remembered Alex, an Italian doctor in his early thirties whose full name was Alessandro

Romano. "Are the nurses the same ones? I hardly saw the senior nurse. Can't remember her name."

"Gwen Sumner, yes, she seems to have settled in for the long haul, and Bernard and Brigitte will also be there. I'm glad because we get on so well." At that moment, Sarah's phone rang. "Excuse me." She pressed the call answer icon. "Hello? Oh hello, Bernard, we were just talking about you. What? Oh no! Will he be alright?

Okay. Yes, I can do that. I should be there soon – hang on a minute, Bernard—

How long before we arrive, Mr Prince?"

"We're approximately an hour away," answered Rachel's father.

"Should be there in about an hour." Sarah went back to the phone call. "Missed you too – will do. See you soon." Sarah frowned as she put her mobile away. "He sends his love."

"What's happened?"

"Brigitte's been called home to Dijon. Her father's been involved in a car accident and needs an operation, but he won't go for surgery until he's seen Brigitte."

"Will he be alright?"

"Bernard says they are not sure, and Brigitte left in a hurry early this morning, so I guess we won't know for a while."

"Oh dear, poor Brigitte. I was looking forward to meeting her properly on this cruise, but I hope he'll be alright. Does that mean you'll be short staffed?"

"Yes and no. There's a new nurse the cruise line has called out of induction so she'll get a baptism of fire. Sorry for the pun, Mr Prince. I'll need to help Bernard in the passenger lounge today, though, so won't be easing myself back into things."

"Oh well. At least they found a replacement in plenty of time," Rachel's father said.

"Yes, that's true, and you don't have to worry about me. I'll be happy in my lap of luxury," agreed Rachel.

"You mean in the gym!"

They all chuckled. Rachel felt inwardly disappointed as she had hoped to spend some quality time with Sarah, but understood that her friend had a job to do.

"That's all you need, first day back," she said light-heartedly.

"I guessed we might be busy, but wasn't expecting things to kick off quite so soon. At least Bernard will still be there."

"Is Bernard the nurse from the Philippines?" asked Rachel's father.

"Yes, he's from Manila. At least I've just enjoyed three months lounging around. I'm sorry I didn't see more of Rachel, but Mum misses me terribly when I'm away and she had sixteen trips planned for when I got home." Sarah rolled her eyes.

Rachel had also missed seeing Sarah and wanted to talk through what had happened with the stabbing and threats made by Tansley, but that would have to wait. They had spoken briefly when they'd snatched time together, but not since the threats.

The car arrived at Southampton docks and Rachel's dad drove towards the cruise terminals.

"You can take the lane on the right, Mr Prince. I'll show my crew pass to the security guards," directed Sarah.

They bypassed queues of traffic already building and pulled up outside the terminal where the magnificent *Coral Queen* was docked. Rachel got out of the car and showed her ticket to the port side crew. The crew quickly and efficiently removed the luggage from the car and stacked Rachel's on to mega-sized luggage trolleys.

Sarah showed her crew pass and grabbed her suitcase and bags before turning to Rachel. "I'll catch you later, Rachel. I need to walk along the port side to the crew entrance. Thank you for the lift, Mr Prince."

"You're welcome. Have a good journey – I'll tell your parents I delivered you safely."

Rachel hugged Sarah and then turned to her father. "Thanks, Dad. Here in plenty of time! Perhaps as well we left early." She kissed him on the cheek.

"Bye, Rachel. Stay safe, we'll see you soon."

Rachel watched her dad drive away before turning and entering the passenger terminal. This year she had a VIP passenger ticket and should be able to bypass the queues and go straight on board. She smiled, thinking of last year when she was a cruise virgin. She now felt like a seasoned cruiser and was looking forward to shopping in New York. Despite the slight setback with Sarah, she was determined to enjoy herself and take full advantage of the opportunity.

Bring it on.

Chapter 4

So much for boarding quickly, thought Rachel, finding herself jammed behind a sizeable fractious party checking in via the VIP entrance. Rachel watched the crowd advancing slowly ahead. They were speaking a foreign language that sounded Eastern European, but it wasn't clear where exactly until she made out a few words of Russian. A large Russian population had based itself in Leeds, and police personnel who wanted to go up through the ranks were encouraged to learn at least one other language, so Rachel had picked up a smattering of Russian. It helped if the suspects didn't realise they might be understood.

The group moved through security at a snail's pace with many demonstrating their displeasure. An English man, clearly the tour guide for the increasingly disgruntled group, worked his way through the crowd, explaining they would need to co-operate fully with security up ahead to speed up the process.

When he spotted Rachel, he asked, "Would you like to go ahead, Miss? We might be a while."

"If the party doesn't mind, then yes, please – otherwise I am happy to wait."

The guide spoke in fluent Russian to another man who appeared to be in charge to check whether it was okay to let her through first.

The man answered, "*Da.*"

"My brilliant command of Russian tells me that was a yes," said Rachel.

The man acknowledged her with a smile. "Follow me, and I will take you to the front of the line." He had obviously picked up some American colloquialisms as well as Russian. The British rarely use the term 'a line' for a queue.

Rachel followed him through the crowd. He looked aged late thirties. Short in stature, around five foot six, he was of slim build with thinning brown hair and slightly bulging dark-blue eyes. Wearing a grey suit with a white shirt and blue tie, he also wore a badge stating his first name, *Thomas,* and his company, *Ronson Tours*. As a policewoman, Rachel had processed this information automatically within seconds. It was all part of the rigorous training from probationer days.

Rachel felt eyes boring through the back of her head as the crowd parted to allow her through. The women looked around ten years younger than the majority of their male counterparts and were lavishly dressed in expensive-looking designer clothes. Most of them also wore high heels. Rachel guessed from previous experience that the long walk up through the tunnels and gangways to board the ship might cause some of the women to regret their choice of footwear.

"Here we are, Miss." Thomas stopped at the front of the queue.

"Thank you," said Rachel, smiling at him sympathetically, acknowledging he could be in for a long day. The group members were becoming increasingly boisterous the longer they had to wait.

"There is a problem with one of the scanners," Thomas explained.

Rachel was called forward by a security guard to pass through the entrance. Once through the scanners, she heard a huge roar of approval. The second scanner was now working and Thomas's group moved through.

Rachel walked uphill along the enclosed makeshift gangway, surrounded by members of the Russian tour group, barely understanding a word as they chattered away happily.

Not that good at Russian then.

They looked wealthy and walked with an air of self-indulgent superiority that suggested they were used to getting what they wanted. The mixture of strong but expensive perfume was at times overwhelming in the enclosed space – although a scent of Estée Lauder's *White Linen* felt more reassuring as it was her mum's favourite.

Once on board, Rachel was offered a glass of champagne. Taking a flute from the waiter, she ambled towards one of the food courts open to passengers, her stomach complaining over missed breakfast. There were a few others who had also boarded the ship early milling around – most people were not meant to arrive until after midday, although Sarah explained that the vast majority arrived earlier. As long as the disembarkation of passengers from the previous cruise had gone smoothly, people were allowed to board to wait in one of the many communal areas until their rooms were ready.

After eating a shrimp salad and finishing the champagne, Rachel moved into one of the lounges and sat people watching for a short time. The Russian group gradually filed through, and Rachel spent some time counting them, getting to twenty before estimating it was a group of around thirty people in total, with stragglers still making their way on board. After becoming tired of watching them, she texted her father to let him know she was safe before calling Carlos.

"Hello, Rachel, I miss you already." Carlos answered the phone immediately.

"You don't see me that often and I only left you yesterday. You can't be missing me."

"Yes, I know, beautiful, but it's different because you're leaving the country."

"I'll be back before you realise I've gone." She smiled as his landline rang in the background.

"Sorry, darling, better answer this. I'm expecting a call – enjoy your trip and think of me. *Ciao*."

"Bye, see you soon."

Rachel smiled again like a Cheshire cat after the call ended. They were not at the 'I love you' stage yet, but Carlos really had been a godsend over the past year. He was supportive without being suffocating and allowed her to be herself, something that her ex had never done. She hadn't grasped how stifling that relationship had been until she was able to look back objectively. Carlos was not at all stifling; rather, he was romantic while allowing her space. He had been her rock over the past six months and she wanted to reciprocate after this holiday.

Rachel spotted Sarah passing through the lounge, now dressed in an officer's uniform, heading towards the gangway leading to the passenger terminal. Sarah smiled and waved before making her way briskly towards the exit. Rachel stood up to stretch her legs and almost bumped into someone.

"Here you are again."

The voice came from behind and she turned to see Thomas standing there. She looked down because of their height difference.

"I'm not sure I introduced myself, my name's Thomas."

"Yes, I know, you're wearing a name badge. I'm Rachel," she replied.

Thomas looked down at his lapel sheepishly. "Whoops, I forget I'm wearing it most of the time. Are you travelling alone, Rachel?" His enquiry appeared sincere rather than a chat-up line, although it wasn't always easy to tell the difference.

"Not really. I have a friend who works on board and I've met a few of the crew before."

"If you would like to join any of our activities, please do. No offence, but a pretty face would brighten up my days. This could be a challenging cruise."

Coming from anyone else, this line would have annoyed Rachel, but Thomas appeared to be earnest in his request, although he might have worded it differently. She was used to men complimenting her beauty, but often wished they would just talk to her without bringing it up all the time.

"I'll bear that in mind, as long as you don't mention the pretty face bit again," she said firmly.

"Okay, it's a deal. Here's a list of our activities. Please join us for any of the ones that take your fancy."

Rachel took the piece of paper and looked at the long list, feeling rather sorry for Thomas. "Surely you're not expected to attend all these!"

"No," he chuckled, "just the ones with the initials *TG* next to them. Thomas Gabriel, at your service, ma'am. The cruise director has allocated members of the entertainment crew to run a lot of them. My job's just to keep the guests happy so they don't fall out or get bored." He leaned closer. "They are stinking rich – one of them is a Russian oligarch," he whispered. "There's also a diplomat among them, a group of businessmen, and lots of WAGs. I don't know who's who myself yet."

Rachel knew WAGs referred to *wives and girlfriends*. It would be intriguing to learn more about this interesting group; she was wavering, wondering what to ask Thomas. At that moment, one of the women called him away.

This cruise is going to be interesting besides relaxing, Rachel thought as the announcement for passengers to make their way to their staterooms whenever they were ready came over the ship's speakers. Opting to head up to her luxury suite on deck fifteen, she tucked the programme away in her handbag, deciding to look at it later.

I might well take Thomas up on his offer.

Chapter 5

Sarah and Bernard checked the passenger health questionnaires and were satisfied the results raised no concerns about a potential norovirus (Norwalk) outbreak. They returned to the ship through security, and on the way Bernard brought her up-to-speed with all the latest crew gossip.

"Guess what? I found out why Gwen asked for a transfer from the last ship," he boasted.

"Okay, I suppose you're going to tell me – so why?"

"She had a fliiiiing with the chief medical officer. Well, a bit more than a fling, actually, on Gwen's side. When she realised it was going nowhere and he wouldn't be leaving his wife, she worried about losing her job if news got out, so asked for a transfer."

"Wow! That I would never have imagined. Gwen seems so quiet and demure. Poor woman. And how – may I ask – did you manage to wheedle that information out of her?"

"Stingers!" Bernard looked overly pleased with himself. A stinger was his own special mix of spirits, a recipe he kept a closely guarded secret, refusing to tell anyone what went into the toxic cocktail. Sarah had sampled a glass once but, after the hideous burning sensations akin to swallowing acid had set her throat on fire, had vowed never to touch one again. The only recognisable spirit in the drink was vodka, but she had no idea what else it contained.

"I'm surprised she's still alive."

"Now, now – you know how everybody loves my special cocktail."

"Not exactly everyone," Sarah protested.

"Okay, not everyone," Bernard continued his bragging. "But ever since then, Gwen's been putty in my hands."

He rubbed his hands gleefully. Sarah looked sceptical – unable to imagine the Australian senior nurse being putty in anyone's hands.

"You wish!" She nudged Bernard good naturedly.

They arrived at the medical centre in good humour. Gwen greeted Sarah, who found it difficult to conceal a smirk when looking at the boss.

"Welcome back, Sarah."

"Thank you, it's good to be back. I'm so sorry to hear about Brigitte's father."

"Yes, it's a sad situation, but let's hope for the best."

Sarah noted Gwen seemed happier and more settled than when they'd worked together previously. *Perhaps Bernard's stingers had a wider effect than expected.*

"Where's the new girl?" asked Bernard, mischievously. As he did so a tall, dour looking woman, skinny with cropped light-brown curly hair, dark green eyes and a wannabe attractive freckled face, entered the office. The woman's appearance was just how Sarah imagined the girl *George* from the *Famous Five* books would have looked, except more austere and a lot older – mid-to-late thirties, Sarah surmised.

"This is Lauren, our new nurse who has stepped in at short notice to help us out," announced Gwen. "Lauren's from Connecticut in the United States, but has been working in Africa for the past two years. Prior to that, she worked in emergency rooms – casualty to you Brits, Sarah. Lauren, meet Sarah and Bernard, your new colleagues."

Sarah smiled and attempted to shake hands. The other woman took the proffered hand, but dropped it again all too quickly.

"Hi, welcome aboard, good to have you with us. Bernard's a tease, so don't let him get to you," Sarah said.

"Hi," said Lauren, not offering any other words. Sarah looked at Bernard for help.

"Yes, I'm Bernard, at your service, ma'am. Anything you need to know – I'm your man." Lauren did smile at Bernard – almost flirtatiously, Sarah observed.

Strange girl, I do hope this won't be a difficult colleague. Ship life's too confined to work with troublesome personalities.

Gwen interrupted Sarah's train of thought. "Lauren's already met Graham and Alex, but will need a tour of the ship. I've explained the uniform policy and put her in Brigitte's room for now. The ship is full to the brim and we have six full days at sea, so I don't need to tell you how busy we'll be. Lauren is very experienced, so once she's familiar with the ship and its procedures, she won't need babysitting."

Thank goodness for that.

Bernard groaned in response to Gwen's announcement regarding the number of passengers on board. "It's been hard without you, Sarah. Now we have to do without Brigitte. Sorry, no offence." He looked at Lauren, who appeared to be somewhere else. Sarah wasn't even sure the woman had heard what Bernard said.

Gwen ended the meeting. "Meds are all stocked up – surgery starts straight after the emergency passenger drill. Bernard, can you show Lauren around the ship and explain where to go and what to do when on call? You're on call, Sarah. You've had quite enough holiday."

She laughed. This was the first time Sarah had seen Gwen laugh out loud, and it made her look much younger and more attractive. The senior nurse was older than the rest of them – early forties, Sarah thought – and had always played the congenial but aloof boss. She never joined in socially with the rest of the team, but considering the background Sarah had just discovered, it was not hard to understand why. Pleased that Gwen seemed relaxed, because it occurred to Sarah that Lauren might not know the meaning of the word, she felt at home already. She'd recently turned twenty-six, and her mother hoped she'd settle down once the travel bug was out of her system, but there was no hurry to comply.

Shortly after their gathering, once Bernard and Lauren had left, Graham came rushing through the entrance to the medical centre, beaming, and enveloped her in a bear hug.

"Sarah, it's good to have you back. We were almost the *A Team* again, weren't we, Sister?" He winked at Gwen.

"Almost." There was that laugh again.

Oh, this is going to be a great cruise. Perhaps Lauren will chill out once she gets used to us all and we can have some fun.

"What do you make of our new girl?"

"Only just met her, she seems fine," replied Sarah, tactfully.

"It might take a little while to adjust – the poor woman's been working in emergency hospitals in Mali where there's a humanitarian crisis. I expect Lauren's seen things hard to imagine, but by all accounts, she is a very capable nurse. I called the lead doctor from the aid organisation and he spoke highly of her capabilities."

Graham Bentley, the chief medical officer, always saw the best in people. An attractive man in his late fifties, he reminded Sarah of her own father. Standing at six foot tall, he kept himself fit, and the only signs of ageing were a few lines around his eyes and a slight paunch. Sarah immediately had guilt pangs about the negative opinion she'd already formed about her new colleague and determined to be a friend to Lauren.

"Well, catch you all later, I have an officers' drill to attend after the passenger drill. Alex is doing evening surgery with you. Call me if you need me." Graham left the office, chipper as ever, with a bounce in his step.

Sarah felt even happier to be back on board the *Coral Queen* after Graham's affectionate display, although it wouldn't be the same without Brigitte. It had been great to have a holiday, but there was nothing like nursing – she loved the job and preferred working on a cruise ship to anywhere else.

It was back to reality now, though. No sooner had Gwen handed over the emergency radio than a call came through to attend to a crew member in engineering who was reportedly light-headed. Sarah made her way down a deck to the mainly metallic area from where the main engines rumbled.

The man she had been called to attend to was Russian and didn't speak much English, but fortunately he had a friend to interpret. The other man, who introduced himself as Erik, shouted above the noise.

"He has light head for past few hours. He doesn't speak much English, but understands what you say." Sarah suspected Erik was Russian too. Knowing the patient's name already from the call out information, she was ready to carry out an assessment.

"Do you have any pain, Mr Popov?" Sarah also shouted.

Popov shook his head and said something to his friend.

"He says, please to call him Jefgeny."

"Okay, Jefgeny."

Jefgeny looked pale even though it was difficult to examine him properly with the dim lighting in this part of engineering. Sarah checked his vital signs and blood pressure; all seemed normal.

"Do you have any chest pain?"

Jefgeny shook his head.

"Is the room spinning or do you just feel weak?"

The man spoke in Russian again and Erik replied, "No spinning, just light head and weakness."

"When did you last eat, Jefgeny?" she asked.

Jefgeny again spoke in Russian and Erik explained that he had not eaten since breakfast. "We have been fixing a problem with pumps," Erik said.

"Well, unless you want him to pass out, I suggest you send someone to get him some food and a hot drink with plenty of sugar." Sarah reached into the medical bag and handed Jefgeny some dextrose tablets. "These should help you feel better for now. I'm making you an appointment to attend surgery at 10am tomorrow for a blood test." She looked at Erik. "Does he understand?"

They both nodded. "*Da*," Jefgeny replied.

Sarah was satisfied it was nothing immediately serious – the engineering crew worked long hours in cramped conditions, and although it was difficult to be certain in the dim lights, she suspected Jefgeny might be anaemic, which would throw up other health concerns.

Dragging the emergency bag around obstacles, she felt every step, a stark reminder of how heavy it could be, but it had to accompany her when she was on call. She'd also forgotten how limited the space was in parts of engineering. This was the worst place on the ship when she was trying to treat people in a serious emergency because the corridors were so narrow, and parts were below the waterline, illuminated only by artificial light. Some areas could only be accessed via makeshift steps akin to loft ladders, and then through tight hatches, creating access difficulties at the best of times.

In this part of engineering, there were huge pipes and little space. It was similar to working on a submarine, she imagined, but a lot louder. Every sound was exaggerated, echoing backwards and forwards from the metal walls and floors.

Sarah decided to take the crew lift back up to deck two and the medical centre. Bernard and Lauren arrived back shortly afterwards, and she acknowledged them while continuing to restock her emergency bag.

Bernard spoke. "Busy already?"

"Yes, a Russian crewman in engineering, with low blood sugar. Should be okay, but I've asked him to come to clinic tomorrow morning for blood tests. He seemed pale – not that I could be certain in the dim lighting."

"I know what you mean. We've just come from engineering, met a few of the crew – everyone seemed alright, so you must have worked your magic."

"This is a huge ship, but I expect I'll soon find my way around." Lauren spoke for the first time, smiling at Bernard. Sarah watched the exchange with interest as Bernard seemed oblivious to the potential overtures of this rather strange new colleague.

"It takes a while. I kept getting lost during my first few weeks, particularly when on call, but we're here if you need help, and—"

"Can I see your notes?" asked Lauren, cutting Sarah off mid-sentence. Sarah handed her the written version of the records that would be typed on to the computerised medical system as soon as possible.

"Crew members receive free treatment courtesy of the cruise line, but you still have to account for every item used so that fresh supplies can be ordered when we're next in port."

Showing a sudden surge of interest, Lauren asked to see how the notes were added to the computer. Sarah brought up Jefgeny Popov's record and noted that he was listed as a US citizen, aged forty with no significant medical history. It seemed odd he didn't speak English, Sarah thought, but maybe he had only recently been granted citizenship.

"He may have succumbed to the scourge of cruise ship life, the habit of drinking too much alcohol – a trap many of the crew fall into," said Sarah while typing in the record. Lauren spent her time glancing at the record before her interest fell away as quickly as it had appeared.

The ship had set sail while Sarah was in engineering. They heard the announcement calling all passengers and crew to muster stations for the emergency drill.

"Here we go." Sarah smiled at the others as they made their way up to the passenger decks, dragging the emergency bag behind her, just in case.

Chapter 6

Rachel danced into the suite, twirling round and round. Her exuberance increased as she remembered the complimentary internet access, an obvious bonus because she could email Carlos while travelling. She grinned from ear to ear every time Carlos came to mind.

A knock at the door interrupted her blissful reverie. She opened it, delighted to discover the smart butler from the previous cruise would be attending to her. They had met after the captain had upgraded her for a few days towards the end of the cruise. Mario was from El Salvador and sounded Spanish.

Not surprising as Spanish is the national language of El Salvador.

"Hello, Miss Rachel." He entered, carrying her suitcase and other baggage. "It's good to meet you again. This year you will have relaxing cruise, yes?"

"That's the plan, Mario." The tall, thin butler was immaculately dressed with short, slick black hair that was well groomed, waves trained to be flat and shiny with the help of hair gel. After asking about his family, who lived in San Salvador, Rachel enquired, "Who is in the other suite?" There were two luxury suites, attended to by a single butler, at the rear of deck fifteen, one on port side and one on the starboard side. Rachel was occupying the starboard suite.

"That one is occupied by rich Russian and girlfriend. The whole corridor on port side to midships is occupied by Russian tour party," Mario said in broken English. "They wanted your suite too for diplomat but had to settle for superior balcony.

They didn't want to be on different decks."

"Oh." Rachel pondered this information, not that keen about the possibility of bumping into Thomas regularly, but she was reassured he would at least use the opposite corridor. "Do you know which room their tour guide is in?"

"No, miss, but I can ask Grace, their stateroom attendant, when we meet later on, if you would like me to."

"Yes please, we met earlier – I would rather not bump into him too often on this deck, if it's possible to avoid it."

"Don't worry, Miss Rachel, I will find out. Is there anything you would like at the moment, Miss Rachel?"

"No, thank you. I'm sure you have plenty to do with your Russian guest."

Mario raised his eyebrows and shrugged his shoulders with a *c'est la vie* smile, leaving her to unpack.

The phone rang in the room. "Hello."

Sarah's voice could be heard among clanging in the background. "Hello, Rachel. Are you all settled in?"

"Yes, just unpacking. What about you?"

"Great to be back, but busy already. I can meet you after surgery this evening, if that suits?"

"Yes, that would be wonderful. Name the place and time and I'll be there."

"Jazz bar around eight o'clock?"

"Yep, see you then."

They said goodbye and hung up.

Rachel looked around, admiring the luxury suite. There was a huge bedroom with a queen-sized bed, a separate sitting room, a large bathroom with bathtub and shower. The rooms were elaborate, but tastefully decorated in pastels with exquisite artwork hanging on the walls. A large flat-screen TV was suspended above her bed, and another one hung on the wall of the sitting room. A welcome bottle of champagne sat on ice, but that could wait for another day.

After unpacking, Rachel walked out on to the balcony overlooking the dark-blue sea behind the ship to watch their departure, and she became lost, admiring the linear patterns made by the surf in the aftermath of the gigantic vessel cutting it apart. They stretched back for miles. The ship carried over three thousand passengers and two thousand eight hundred crew. Sarah called it a small city.

Rachel watched Southampton becoming a dot in the distance as they sailed away. The announcement came over the ship's loudspeakers, requesting passengers attend the compulsory emergency drill. Rachel left the room, but not before taking a quick glance into the rear corridor to check it was clear. She didn't mind coming across Thomas later, but would rather do it on her own terms until her suspicions that he was harmless were confirmed.

After dinner, Rachel sauntered along to the jazz bar where she and Sarah had arranged to meet up. The sound of a lively jazz band filled the air, and the room was already filling up with cheerful passengers. Her friend sat at a small round table by a window.

Sarah looked elegant, even in her officer's uniform. Rachel noticed she was armed with the large emergency bag and a glass of lemonade sat on the table.

"You're on call already then?"

Sarah stood and hugged her. "Yes, I drew the short straw, but can't complain because the others have been on call regularly over the past few months. Apologies in advance, I might get called away at any moment. We've already been busy." Sarah lowered her voice. "I've ordered you a glass of red, but as you can see, I'm on the soft stuff."

Rachel didn't ask any questions about her work as they were surrounded by other passengers. A waiter appeared, bringing Rachel's wine and setting it on the table with a small bowl of nibbles. Rachel thanked him.

"Thanks. I'll take any time I can get with you and be glad." She smiled at Sarah. "Have you eaten?"

"Yes, Raggie, the medical team steward, brought us food at the end of surgery. I think you met him last year. Did you have a luxurious dinner?"

"I did meet him, a lovely man from what I remember, and yes, my dinner was delicious. The chefs excelled themselves."

"What are your table companions like?"

"They seem pleasant enough, but won't be able to live up to last year's." Rachel grinned, remembering the lovely people she had met on the previous cruise.

"There's a family of four who chatted amongst themselves, an older Canadian couple in their seventies, myself, and a quiet elderly man who's seated next to me."

Sarah laughed out loud. "I suspect Carlos phoned the maître d' to ensure that was the case!" Rachel joined in with her friend's laughter. "I'm on call until tomorrow night, so we won't be able to meet up tomorrow. Will you be alright?"

"Yes, don't worry about me. I'll go to the chapel service first thing, and afterwards will find some mischief to get up to. In fact, I met a tour guide leading a Russian group. He gave me their itinerary with an open invitation to join in with any of the activities."

"Oh, lucky you – how do you do it? Is this tour guide hoping for anything in return?" Sarah's brow furrowed.

"No, I don't believe he is – he seems harmless enough. He said he needs a distraction from the tour group. In fact, they're all on the same deck as me, but thankfully on the opposite side. A Russian oligarch's in the other luxury suite, with the rest of his party filling the rooms in that corridor."

"Sounds like you will have an interesting time. We're aware of that group because they've already insisted that Graham check up on one woman's blood pressure tonight. Three of them have also forgotten to bring prescribed medication with them, so he'll need to sort that out too. He might have his work cut out on this voyage."

"Poor Dr Bentley," said Rachel. "From what I witnessed as they were boarding, they could be quite a demanding group of people."

"Oh well, it makes for interesting cruising – never a dull moment," sighed Sarah. "Graham will have met worse and takes it all in his stride."

"Well, I will take the kind Thomas up on his offer, having taken a quick glance through their itinerary. They are doing a tour of engineering tomorrow. I'd love to explore life below the waterline, as you call it!"

"Small world, I've been down to engineering myself this afternoon." At that moment, Sarah's bleep went off, and she reached for her radio. "Sorry, Rachel, I have to go – speak tomorrow." She walked away, talking into the radio.

"Bye, hope it's not too busy," said Rachel, deciding to finish her glass of red wine before heading back upstairs to her stateroom.

Day 1

Chapter 7

"Jefgeny Popov!" Sarah called the name out in the medical centre waiting room. No-one came forward. "You can lead a horse to water, but you can't make it drink," she murmured to herself as she retired to the clinic room to look up the next patient on the list.

Surgery flew past as she saw a mixture of passengers and crew with various ailments and injuries. Sarah was dog-tired after being up most of the night on calls to passengers with minor scrapes, mostly due to too much alcohol. One lady called her out at 11pm having forgotten to bring her blood pressure tablets, so Sarah had supplied her with a pack from the treatment room. Typical first night calls, really. Medication given to passengers was recorded in a logbook, and then the cruise line charged passengers or their insurance companies for both the medicine and the consultation with a doctor or nurse on board.

With morning surgery finished, Sarah joined the other medical staff in Gwen's office for coffee.

"Well, that was a busy one." Graham joined them after seeing the final passenger attending surgery. "Is everyone okay?"

They all responded in the affirmative.

"Busy, but not complicated," said Bernard. "Lauren managed every condition without my help. I just sat back and admired her remarkable expertise." He smiled at the new girl.

"That's not quite true, I needed your help at least three times." She grinned back at him.

"Good to see you settling in," cut in Graham before the mutual admiration society had the chance to continue.

"Thank you, sir," Lauren responded.

"No need for the sir here. Call me Graham when we are staff only and Dr Bentley in front of passengers and other crew."

"Yes, sir – sorry, Graham."

Sarah was kicking herself for finding it so difficult to take to Lauren, so she made an attempt to get to know her. "Why don't you join us for lunch in the company dining room, Lauren?" she invited.

"Yes do," added Bernard. "Are you guys coming?" he asked the rest of the team.

"I'll be working on accounts – the bills are piling up already," answered Gwen.

"I've got to meet with the captain to give him an update," said Graham. "Alex, you need to deal with that problem downstairs."

"What problem?" enquired Sarah.

"A crewman was found dead in his cabin this morning. Poor fellow, looks like he had a heart attack in his sleep. Alex confirmed death first thing and called me. We left him there until we could bring him quietly to the morgue."

Sarah baulked at the reminder that they had a morgue on board the ship.

"Oh dear, that's sad. Who was it?"

"The man worked in engineering, according to the roommate. He hasn't needed a doctor since boarding ship. Medical application form unremarkable and pre-cruise check-ups were fine."

All crew members, including doctors and nurses, had to have a medical evaluation on land, which included lengthy form-filling, blood tests, X-rays and a physical examination, before stepping foot on a cruise ship. Medical evaluations cost a small fortune in some countries, but it was important from the cruise line's perspective to have healthy employees on board ship because Queen Cruises accepted responsibility for funding the medical care of the crew, and repatriation on account of illness or death, once they were aboard.

"What's his name?" enquired a concerned Sarah. "I met a man called Jefgeny Popov in engineering yesterday and made an appointment for him to come to clinic this morning, but he didn't show."

"The dead guy was called Erik Marinov," Alex answered, "but it was a roommate called Jefgeny who found him. They shared the room, but Jefgeny worked until 2am after swapping shifts with another crewman. When he got back, he assumed his friend was sleeping. On discovering him dead this morning, he called for a medic. After I confirmed Mr Marinov was dead, Jefgeny was in considerable distress, but I couldn't get much out of him. I'm just heading back down to deck C now."

"Erik interpreted for Jefgeny yesterday – he looked fit and healthy. Something worried me about Jefgeny's health, not Erik's. That explains why he didn't show up this morning. Can I join you, Alex? I'd like to find out how Jefgeny is."

"Yes sure. Come on, let's go. Do you want to come too, Lauren?"

"No thanks, I'll keep Bernard company."

Sarah raised her eyebrows, but Lauren didn't notice. Bernard shrugged his shoulders behind Lauren's back and grinned. Sarah put her tongue out at him and followed Alex down to the decks below the waterline where crew members had their cramped berths. The berths were still comparative luxury for some of the crew compared to what they left behind in their home countries. Sarah appreciated her good fortune, having a room above the waterline as an officer.

There were many decks below, and they walked down three sets of stairs before arriving at the right one. As always, Sarah noticed how the air got stuffier the further down they went. Stale cigarette smoke pervaded the air, making it even worse.

"Blooming cigarettes, I hate coming down here," muttered Alex in a voice barely audible. The bass beat of loud music emanated from some of the rooms where Sarah assumed crew, who worked nights or were on breaks, were enjoying down-time.

They walked single file as the corridors narrowed.

"I can never get used to the noise down here. How can anyone fall asleep?" asked Sarah.

"Sorry, can't hear."

Ignoring Alex's joke, Sarah continued her rant. "Music, if you can call it that, one might manage, but not the engine noises, all these vibrations and other creaks and groans." As if on cue, the rumbling sound of metal assaulted their ears, along with an irritating constant humming noise that Sarah certainly did not find soothing. The din reverberated off the surrounding metal, causing every sound to echo back at them.

"I do know what you mean, but I presume it's sheer exhaustion after twelve to fourteen hour shifts. It's probably no worse than living next to a busy motorway, I guess."

"If you say so." Sarah didn't sound convinced. She couldn't believe how negative she was feeling. "There's no way I would have renewed my contract if I'd had to live down here."

When they arrived at the cabin where the body of Erik had remained while morning surgery took place, she couldn't help thinking how tragic it would be to die in a small, airless cabin. With barely enough room for the two of them – made worse by the dismal darkness – Sarah held her breath as the pungent smells of body odour, dirty washing and stale cigarette smoke invaded her olfactory system. Added to this was the familiar, fetid smell of death all health professionals become accustomed to early in their training. Without a porthole, the cabin seemed unusually dark, despite the light having been left on. The light bulb barely broke through the shadows.

Alex took a quick look around. "We're safe to move him now. Most of the crew are at work – we'll put him on the stretcher and move him to the morgue. I'm glad he slept on the bottom bunk. Poor man looks heavy."

Sarah was hardly listening. She noticed Erik's bags had already been packed and placed in a corner. She looked at the bulky form of Erik, lying on the bottom bunk. Although his skin had taken on an ashen appearance, she recognised him as the man who, just yesterday, had appeared tough and robust when interpreting for his companion.

"He looked so healthy," she murmured.

Alex put a hand on Sarah's shoulder; she was welling up. *What on earth's the matter with me?*

"Graham and I did search for drugs earlier, but discovered nothing. There are no injuries or suicide note. Everything points to him dying in his sleep. Graham agreed that cause of death was probably a heart attack. The security team have been through the place while we've been in surgery, and they too detected nothing untoward."

"Have his family been informed?" Sarah asked.

"Not yet. We've checked his details, and he has a sister in Russia, but no relatives in the USA, despite being an American citizen. The details in his personnel file are sparse, according to the chief security officer. Someone in head office will inform the next of kin."

Sarah sighed. "How tragic, no-one to mourn his loss. Will there be a post mortem?"

"Unlikely – too expensive. The death appears to be natural causes, and with no close relatives to demand answers, he'll probably be cremated in America."

With no sign of Jefgeny, and feeling like she needed to get a grip of herself, Sarah wanted to get away. "Do you need me to help you get him on to the trolley?"

They heard voices in the corridor and two security guards appeared.

"No thanks, these officers are just in time." Alex turned to them. "Come on, guys, let's move this poor man out of here."

Sarah left the crew quarters, a little overwhelmed. Only her second day back after a long break, and she was already tired from lack of sleep. She'd only met

Erik briefly, but his death had come as a shock.

Sarah decided to return to surgery and catch up with paperwork from the morning; she had lost her appetite. Gwen was still in her office with the door open.

"What are you doing back here?" she called.

"I want to finish the paperwork and log items used this morning before taking a break. To be honest, I found it all a bit depressing downstairs."

"You'll get back into the swing of it. You've been thrown in at the deep end, haven't you?"

"I guess so. It was a busy shift so I must be feeling it more than I should."

"If it's any consolation, we all hate it when crew members die on board. We're like a family, even though we don't know everyone, so it's hard to take. But sudden deaths happen on ships as well as on land."

"I know, it's just that he doesn't seem to have anyone to grieve his loss, and his bags were all packed, ready to go to the purser's office, as if he never existed." Her eyes filled up again.

"Don't let it get to you. From what I can gather, he had half a dozen close friends who will miss him and grieve for him like family."

Gwen was right. Sarah thought about it and realised she was overreacting. Of course his friends would miss him.

"That reminds me, I must track down Jefgeny Popov. He still needs blood tests, and I think the loss of his roommate will have upset him."

Sarah walked into a clinic room and pulled up Jefgeny's records on her computer, glad of the distraction.

Chapter 8

The chapel was well attended, Rachel thought, considering it was nine o'clock in the morning and people were on holiday. It was to be an interdenominational service conducted by a visiting Baptist minister from a church in New York City.

A buxom bleach-blonde woman in her sixties sat next to Rachel. "I only came to meet the captain," she whispered.

"He's not here," replied Rachel.

"Just my luck," she grunted, but stayed anyway.

The pastor explained how he got to cruise regularly for free, in return for performing ministerial duties on board Queen Cruises. "Marriages," he explained, "are almost always performed by the captain or his deputy, though."

"Blast, looks like I'll have to find hubby number five." The woman next to Rachel nudged her.

"Number five?" Rachel mouthed.

"That's the way to do it, dear, hitch, fleece and run!"

Rachel liked this rather vociferous woman, but wasn't sure whether to believe her. If the diamonds adorning her hands and neck were anything to go by, she could well be telling the truth.

With her attention back on the service, Rachel found the bubbly minister made the whole thing fun and his jokes made her laugh. Not quite as much as those of the woman next to her, though. She didn't know all the hymns and choruses, but joined in as well as she could.

Feeling invigorated by the uplifting and entertaining hour, Rachel wandered over to the Voyager lounge where the Russian party would be meeting at 10am, prior to their tour of the engine room.

Recognising some of the men from embarkation, she was beginning to have second thoughts about gate-crashing, and was about to make a discreet exit when she was reassured by Thomas's entrance with a clipboard in hand. He waved enthusiastically, convincing her to join him and the gathering group.

Thomas spoke briefly in Russian to an unhappy looking man, who eventually moved away to join the others.

"Problems?" asked Rachel.

"Not really. A bit of jockeying for position among the ladies, apparently. Nothing too serious. One of the glamorous girlfriends is splitting the ladies off into a splinter group. There's quite a hierarchy among them, and the more senior ladies don't like it, so there might be a row brewing. I've told him, as long as there are no fisticuffs, there's nothing I can do about their internal squabbling, but I'll try to make sure they all enjoy themselves." Thomas grinned at Rachel. "Glad to see you took me up on my offer. It's good to have a pret... sorry, a friendly face."

"That's better, and thank you. I found it hard to resist a tour of the workings down below – it will be interesting to see how it all works."

"Personally, I'd rather be by the pool, but such is life." He sighed. "I need to check everyone is here and give them a tour badge to wear. Here's one for you." Thomas handed over a sticky blue badge with *Guest* printed on it and a pair of earmuffs, which she put around her neck. "We're just waiting for the chief engineer who will be taking us down. Come over, I'll introduce you – there are only ten of the group taking this tour."

Rachel followed Thomas over towards a group of six men who stopped talking as they arrived.

"This is Rachel, a fellow guest who will be joining us for the trip."

"Hello, we remember you from yesterday," said the tall man she had earmarked as the boss the day before. "Boris Stanislav – at your service, I look forward to getting to know you, Rachel."

A tall, well-built man with blond hair, Boris then turned to Thomas. "My father worked for government as naval submarine engineer, so I am very much looking forward to tour."

Rachel discerned an air of authority in Boris. Others in the group held back until they were invited to speak with him. She also noticed two burly men standing back, watching him continuously. One, short and bald with muscles the size of footballs protruding through a tailored black jacket, looked like a baddie straight out of a *Bond* movie. The other man was also powerfully built, but much taller with a head of thick dark-brown hair and a deep scar above his right eye, running the length of his face to his chin. They both looked menacing in a Mafioso way, but also slightly comical as they seemed to move in unison. However, Rachel thought they would make anyone think twice before approaching Boris without permission. She wondered if Boris would turn out to be the oligarch, deciding to ask Thomas when she had the chance.

"We are waiting for the chief engineering officer, Mr Stanislav, and then we'll get moving. There seems to be one missing from the tour group?"

"Who?" asked Boris.

"Mr Nikolai Stepanov."

"No problem, he is here now." They all turned and saw a man who appeared to be late-thirties, with jet black hair, moustache and bright, penetrating sky blue eyes. He was strikingly handsome, in dangerous-looking way.

The man nodded to Boris secretively. "Sorry I'm late, boss, I had to fill out some papers for the business we discussed last evening."

"Yes, yes. Never mind that now. This young lady is called Rachel, and she's joining us for the tour – a friend of Thomas."

The man took Rachel's hand in his and drew it up to his lips while holding her gaze. Rachel thought he had the most captivating smile ever, until she looked into frosty eyes and knew not to trust him.

"Charmed, I'm sure."

Rachel intuitively sensed the false charm; he made her skin crawl. She couldn't move her hand away quickly enough, subconsciously wiping it on the back of her trousers. Thomas came to her rescue by stepping between them and handing Nikolai a tour badge.

"Mr Stepanov, please wear this for our tour." He then took Rachel's arm and led her away. "Be careful of him," he whispered. "There's something about him that gives me the creeps."

"Me too. Thanks for the heads up, but I have no intention of letting Mr Stepanov anywhere near me."

"Good. Oh, at last!" Thomas turned in the direction of the door as two officers in bright, shiny whites entered the lounge. One of them, who Rachel assumed was the chief engineer, had four gold stripes on shoulder epaulettes.

"I'm not late, am I?" The officer looked at his watch.

"No, you're right on time," answered Thomas. "We are all present and correct with one extra." He gestured towards Rachel.

"Please could you let me have your name and stateroom number, madam?" Wearing a name badge with Steven Rafferty on it, the officer had a Scottish accent.

"It's Rachel Prince," she replied, surreptitiously showing him a card with her stateroom number on it while Thomas busied himself with Boris.

"Just a precaution, Ms Prince. Thank you." The officer moved away and spoke into his radio. Obviously receiving a satisfactory answer, he turned almost immediately and rejoined them.

"Good morning, everyone. Welcome aboard the *Coral Queen*. I am the chief engineering officer and this is one of my engineering officers, Ramjeet Singh. You will need to follow me at all times. Please be aware that conditions in some of the areas we will pass through are a bit cramped and you will need to walk in single file. Please do not leave the group at any time during this tour. I will lead the group and Officer Singh will bring up the rear. If you have any questions, I request that you ask them at the end of the tour and do not distract any of the workers from their jobs – if you want to get to New York on time." He laughed at his own joke and waited for the group to give a polite response. "Please wear the earmuffs you've been given when we enter engineering bays. Away we go then."

He headed towards the door with Boris hot on his heels and the group followed, along with the minders whom Rachel had subconsciously named Tweedledee and Tweedledum. Boris lost no time in picking the chief's brains.

Rachel walked with Thomas, but didn't want to ask too many questions while in such close proximity to the others. None of the Russian women had joined them.

"No women coming along?" she asked Thomas.

She recognised the voice of Nikolai, answering from behind. "Not a woman's tour, Miss Prince. Our women are attending beauty therapy this morning."

Rachel noted the veiled rebuke, but didn't take the bait.

"It's much noisier down here."

As they descended a number of different stairwells, so the sounds grew louder. Rachel slowed down in order to let Nikolai pass, but he stuck like glue. Unfortunately Thomas, distracted by others in the group, was unable to come to her aid again, being near the front and barely visible.

The corridors narrowed, and they moved along in single file so crew members could pass if they needed to. Tweedledee and Tweedledum remained close to Boris, who remained immediately behind the chief as far as Rachel managed to see, but an ever-increasing gap was emerging between the front and the rear of the group. Rachel sensed this was deliberate as the man immediately ahead of her was walking at a slower than natural pace.

The final member of the group ahead disappeared as he turned left. As Rachel's group turned the corner, she almost bumped into the man in front as he stopped abruptly. The straggler of the first group appeared to have been talking hurriedly to a crew member, but he stopped as soon as they arrived and continued on his way. The crew member, looking frightened, scurried past them as if he had seen a ghost.

"Hurry along, please," Officer Singh called from the rear, sounding frustrated. The man in front of her picked up his pace. Irritated by Nikolai getting ever closer behind her, she broke away.

They reached a pair of large metal doors, where Rachel finally made her escape from Nikolai, entering what appeared to be the main engine room. The noise sounded much louder as the engines thundered to new heights, making it difficult to hear anything. The humongous chains from the anchor that were wound around a huge metallic crank dominated the room and grabbed the group's attention. The deafening sound became worse, so the majority applied their ear protection.

The chief engineer tried saying something, and as the group gathered closer, he bellowed above the noise, but to no avail. Rachel gathered snippets about how the ship operated and how the anchor was winched up and down when needed – she didn't wish to imagine how loud that would be. Lots of crewmen in dark grey overalls continued their work around them. The room felt hot and airless while the dim lighting caused it to close in on the visitors, but Steven Rafferty seemed perfectly at home here. Apart from the fact he was raising his voice, you would not have known that he was standing in a partially lit tin can.

They moved through to a quieter room, larger and more spacious than the one they'd left. This room was filled with state-of-the-art computers and large glass dials. Officers sat or stood at various sub stations around the room. The group could hear the Chief clearly now.

"This is the main engine room that makes the ship go and is the heart of the vessel." He spoke proudly. The room had a little natural light as a trickle of sunlight came through narrow windows near the ceiling. This area was above the waterline – just!

Before she'd learned very much at all, the tour ended hastily and the guests were escorted back to their original meeting place where the Chief answered various questions. Rachel excused herself, in need of fresh air. Having had her interest piqued, she mulled over what the connection might be between the frightened crew member and the man in the Russian party.

Chapter 9

After eating a hearty lunchtime salad from the buffet, Rachel took a stroll around deck fourteen above the lido deck where people splashed around in the many pools or sunbathed on loungers. The grill bar looked hectic and the smell of burgers and sausages made her hungry again. Rachel liked to keep herself in shape with regular gym workouts and jogging, so she walked past the enticing but deadly part of the deck.

Those things should come with health warnings.

Pausing at one of the side rails, she looked out at the deep blue Atlantic Ocean, appreciating that this would be her view for the next six days. She missed Carlos and decided to return to her room and email him.

"Rachel – where did you disappear to?"
A voice arrested her in her tracks.

"Hello, Thomas. You were busy with
your charges when I left, but I enjoyed the
tour, thanks. I would have tracked you
down later to extend my gratitude."
Rachel felt embarrassed for not having
remained behind to thank Thomas for his
hospitality earlier. Her mind had been
occupied by the puzzling encounter
between the Russian and the crewman.

"Oh, that's no problem – my pleasure.
The Chief made it informative, although a
tad too cramped and noisy down there for
my taste. Anyone who can work there for
a full day with all that racket going on has
my complete admiration and respect."

Rachel took the opportunity to quiz
Thomas. "Yes, incredibly noisy. Did you
see that crewman passing by? He might
have known one of the men in your
group."

"No, can't say I noticed anyone in particular. I suffer from claustrophobia, so was focussed on the person in front of me. Boris kept bombarding the Chief with questions after being specifically asked not to. I thought the Chief was very patient with him. No-one in this group would know a crewman, though, Rachel – they are poles apart. Every one of this party oozes success and wealth – even the bodyguards will be better off than we are."

He laughed. Rachel thought Thomas looked quite wealthy himself in his designer clothing alongside the Rolex on his left wrist, but didn't comment.

Thomas continued, "Maybe they heard someone speaking Russian, as I understood from the Chief there are quite a few Russians working in engineering."

Thomas didn't appear to be hiding anything, and what he said made sense.

Why wouldn't they pass the time of day with one of their own countrymen?

"That's probably it," she answered. "A little mystery cleared up in my head."

"Where are you heading now, Rachel?"

"I'm going back to my room to email my boyfriend."

"A man should have known that one with such exceptional beauty would have a boyfriend somewhere."

"Thomas, stop saying things like that! If I suspect for one moment, you have ulterior motives for inviting me along to the tours—"

"Rachel, relax. I'm sorry, no offence intended. You don't need to worry about me." He looked around nervously, then whispered, "I'm gay – but would rather nobody in the tour party knew that. Russians can be very funny about these things, you know. They've not quite moved into the twenty-first century yet."

"Whoops – so sorry, Thomas, I didn't realise, and of course not. It's none of their business, or mine for that matter. I don't think you're being fair on Russians, though; I'm sure that many of them are very much in tune with the twenty-first century and would have no problem at all with your sexuality."

"Whatever." Thomas smiled cheekily and shrugged.

"Sorry again if I got the wrong end of the stick."

"No worries, I do a good cover-up act after years of practice." He sounded bitter. "I've only recently *come out* and am still getting used to saying it. It sounds ridiculous, but I come from a very macho background – my father was an RAF colonel, as was his father before him. Can you imagine they expected me to follow the family tradition and join up?" He cackled loudly.

"Does your father know?"

"OMG – No! He'd have apoplexy. As it is, he's disappointed that his only son hasn't followed in the family tradition. My mother knows – only told her six months ago when I started to get serious about someone. I dreaded the reaction, but there wasn't one – she said she'd always known. Mothers!" He shrugged his shoulders and continued. "Anyway, enough about me. Why don't you join us later? There's a Salsa lesson at five. I promise to protect you from any amorous Russians." He laughed, seeming more relaxed for having told her his secret.

"I've got your itinerary so will find you if I decide to take you up on your kind offer. Thanks again, Thomas."

"Don't worry about what anyone in the group thinks – Boris made it quite clear that you would be welcome to any of our activities. He believes I fancy you and I didn't put him right." Thomas winked and walked away, wiggling his hips playfully and looking triumphant.

Rachel grinned as she headed back to her room. Thomas was growing on her, and now she felt safe, she would be a lot happier joining in with him and his tour party. Still wary of Nikolai, she would play along with Thomas if required.

Sarah phoned while Rachel was emailing Carlos from her stateroom.

"Hi, Rachel – just checking in. Is everything alright?"

"Yes, everything's fine. I joined the engine room tour this morning – interesting, but I agree with you about the noise. How do people work down there?"

"With difficulty. I've spent more time down there since being back on the ship than I would care to. First seeing a Russian yesterday, and then today his roommate was found dead in the room they shared."

"Oh dear! How tragic. That's all you needed on your second day back. Are you okay?"

"Yes, fine now, but it's all a bit sad. The chap who died doesn't really have any family to speak of, and the only people who will be mourning his loss will be his roommate and his fellow crewmen. He worked in engineering and was one of the guys I met yesterday because he interpreted for his roommate, who didn't speak English."

"Are there any suspicious circumstances? Has security checked it out?" Being a police officer, Rachel had been called to sudden deaths occasionally, and always had to rule out anything suspicious before allowing a body to be moved. Such deaths had to be referred to the coroner and sometimes this resulted in a post-mortem, while others would be discussed with a GP to ask if they were happy to issue a death certificate for natural causes.

"Not this time, Rachel. We're not having any suspicious deaths on this cruise, so you just relax." Sarah sniggered. "Seriously, though, it looked like a heart attack in the night. There's no evidence of drugs or alcohol poisoning, which can occur, and no sign of violence or suicide, so I suspect we're looking at a natural death. Chief Security Officer Waverley, who you will remember from your last cruise, has cleared the room and not found anything suspicious. He will do some background checks on the man and his roommate, but I'm sure there will be nothing untoward."

"That's a relief – I really do want us to relax, and PC Prince would like to enjoy this holiday, but I'm so sorry you've been thrown back in at the deep end. Hopefully the rest of the cruise will be less eventful."

"Let's hope so, and at least you were nowhere near this one! I need to track down his roommate, though, because I'm concerned about him. I've just got back from engineering myself and he seems to be AWOL. He doesn't speak much English at all and he depended on the deceased, Erik, for translation. He's probably found a quiet corner to get drunk in."

"What makes you say that?"

"Well, when I saw him yesterday, even in the dim lighting down in engineering, he looked pale. He was supposed to come to surgery for an appointment this morning for blood tests, but he didn't show. Mostly when crewmen become anaemic, it's due to the excessive alcohol they consume on board, and they develop stomach ulcers or, worst-case scenario, liver cirrhosis. I still want to run those tests."

"Okay, now I get it. You'll be right, then, because the first thing a heavy drinker would do if upset would be to get drunk."

"Except that cruise ship procedure is so stringent. Most of the crew realise when to work and when to play. He'll be lucky if he keeps his job after going missing from shift, although I will ask Graham to fight his corner if he is passed out drunk somewhere."

"Is anyone looking for him?"

"Yes, actively at present – his friends are helping with the search. He went missing in the middle of his shift around midday but nobody reported it until I went looking for him an hour ago. His friends covered for him, hoping he'd come back. Security has been told to keep a lookout. I just hope he hasn't done anything silly."

"Like what?"

"Like throwing himself overboard."
Sarah sounded worried.

"Wait – did you say he went missing at midday? That's when I was on the engineering tour. I saw a crewman looking scared, like he'd seen something frightening, and I'm sure he spoke to one of the members of the tour group, so he could have been Russian."

"Can you describe him?"

"Yes, about six-foot, skinny-looking with clothes hanging off him, and he had bright-red wavy hair and a moustache."

"Wow, Rachel – that's him. Do you know which way he went?"

"Not really, but he went in the opposite direction to the engine room because we were heading towards it. Sarah, he looked terrified. I've got a bad feeling about this."

"Me too – I'd better call Waverley. They'll need to do a ship-wide search.

Are you sure he looked frightened rather than upset?"

"Hard to tell, but I would say he looked like he had just had a fright or a shock. His eyes were darting around and he rushed past rather than walked. The death of his friend could explain it, but I do hope it has nothing to do with the Russian he spoke to in the group."

"I'll call Waverley. My money's on him being in a drunken stupor somewhere below the waterline or in the crew bar, but if not, I'll keep you informed. Shall we meet up again tonight in the jazz bar? This time I'll be off duty."

"Yes, that would be great – see you around nine."

Rachel put the phone down with the distinct impression that yet again, this might be no ordinary cruise. She made up her mind to go to the salsa class and see if there was any more to that chance meeting between the Russian and the crewman in the corridor.

Chapter 10

Sarah put the telephone down after speaking to Waverley for over half an hour. The turn of events had troubled him, it seemed, so he'd responded by being brusque and dismissive. He'd told Sarah in no uncertain terms that he would find Jefgeny Popov within the hour.

"The captain will need to know that things might be more complicated than we first thought, but I don't envision there being any relationship between a chance encounter with Russians in a corridor and Popov going missing," he snorted. "Let's hope your friend Rachel is wrong this time and the man is drunk in a corner somewhere."

"Yes, I'm certain he will be," Sarah replied, although she was anything other than certain.

"The team can make enquiries about this Russian group and carry out discreet background checks, although with diplomats in the party, we may run into problems. You realise that if it wasn't your friend suggesting the crewman looked frightened, I wouldn't be wasting any time on this."

"Yes, Chief, thank you. Perhaps it will be nothing. I'd better get back to work."

Sarah walked into one of the clinic rooms and sat down at a desk. Taking a deep breath, she hoped against hope all would be well with Jefgeny.

Shortly afterwards, the speakers in the medical centre burst into life as the captain made an unscheduled announcement.

"Good afternoon, ladies and gentleman, this is Captain Jenson speaking. The chief engineer has requested we stop the ship for a short while so he can deal with a minor problem in the engine room. I would like to reassure passengers that the problem will not stop the ship from operating at its full capacity, but it is easier to fix with the engines switched off. We are currently in calm seas that will allow us to float without dropping anchor. Please accept my apologies for any inconvenience and rest assured you will be informed once we are due to be underway again. Please continue to take full advantage of all the wonderful facilities and entertainment, and enjoy your cruise aboard the *Coral Queen*. Thank you."

Sarah felt the ship's engines stop. In the silence that followed, it was easy to see they were at a standstill from the porthole in her clinic room.

"Minor problem in engineering indeed!" Graham blustered. Entering the room red faced, he was followed by Alex, Gwen, Bernard and Lauren. "There'd better not be another dead body to deal with."

Sarah heard the strain in his voice and worried about his blood pressure with the stress he was exuding – not like him at all. The medical team was not used to crew deaths, although they were not unheard of. The occasional crew member fell or jumped overboard, but she had not come across this during her first year working for the cruise line. The occasional passenger death was far more likely, particularly on a world cruise due to the number of older people travelling with serious health problems. Despite an increase in younger people taking cruises these days, there remained a disproportionate number of elderly people on every sailing. She had only experienced one passenger death on board, plus the incident the previous year when a death had taken place in one port, but nothing like this.

"Don't worry, Graham, they'll find him off his head in some obscure part of the ship," said Gwen.

"Let's hope so. Anyway, the reason I'm here – Sarah, Gwen, we need to take another peek at the body – captain's orders. Tell me you didn't miss anything, Alex?" What Graham meant was that he hoped neither of them had missed anything.

Alex looked uncomfortable. "As far as I know, I didn't miss anything – there was nothing untoward," he replied, quietly. "Shall I do the passenger visits while you check?"

"Good idea, thanks." Graham calmed down a little.

Sarah saw Alex's head drop as he left and felt sorry for him.

Bernard and Lauren took over from Sarah, checking stocks and sorting out medicines. Sarah and Gwen followed Graham into the morgue. They stood back while Gwen pulled out one of the six shiny steel refrigerated drawers, available to store corpses when deaths occurred on board. This one contained the body of Erik Marinov.

Sarah gasped at the cold draught of air that enveloped them as the drawer opened. Erik was lying on his back, covered only by a plastic sheet that Gwen pulled back. A respectful silence descended, but it produced a macabre atmosphere.

"Dreadful business," muttered Graham. Sarah had never seen him so stressed, but understood his concern that Alex might have made a mistake. They exposed the naked body and Graham began his examination. He scrutinised every part of Erik from the top of his head to the bottom of his feet. "One bruise to his right arm. His roommate said he sustained it during an arm wrestling competition in the crew bar two nights ago."

"To think he was alive and arm wrestling recently, it's tragic," whispered Gwen to Sarah. Sarah nodded, but sensed Graham was not in the mood for chit-chat. He wanted to get his examination done as soon as possible.

He seemed satisfied he had examined the body thoroughly from the front. "Okay, Gwen, Sarah – pull him on to his side please." They did so and Graham repeated the same examination of the rear of Erik's body. "Okay, relax back, please."

They released Erik on to his back and Graham looked relieved. "Thankfully, I can find no evidence of foul play. We can't totally rule out suicide, but there was no evidence of drugs or medication in his room. We are back to probable cause of death as a heart attack."

It was as the condensation from the refrigerator cleared around the body that Sarah's attention was drawn to something else. She scrutinised a small birthmark on Erik's upper left arm that revealed a faint mark in the centre.

"What is it, Sarah?" Graham snapped.

"Erm, not sure. Would you take a look, please?"

Graham shot around to her side and examined the birthmark too. "I can't make it out. Gwen, can you get me a magnifying glass, please?" Gwen left the morgue and Graham stared at Sarah. "My God, I hope this isn't what I think it is."

They were silent as Gwen returned to the room and handed over the magnifying glass. Graham squinted with furrowed brow as he checked the mark, but they all realised what it was: a tiny speck from a needle carefully concealed within the darker part of the birthmark. The team were puzzled about what might have been injected into Erik's arm, but there was little doubt what it meant.

This was murder.

"Not a word to anyone outside the medical team – except to your friend, Sarah. This is not getting out, at least not until I've discussed it with the captain and the chief of security. We'll keep it from the new girl, too – we don't know yet whether she can be discreet enough to keep this under wraps. I would prefer to keep it as quiet as possible."

Graham marched out of the room with Gwen hot on his heels. Sarah stayed behind to close the drawer containing the late Erik.

"Sorry, Erik, we didn't realise, but we know what happened now. I'm positive security will find who did this to you."

Sarah had a sinking feeling that something awful had also happened to Jefgeny – unless, of course, he had committed the murder, which might also explain his disappearance. She couldn't believe he would have harmed his friend, though; they had seemed close.

Perhaps he suspects it was murder, or worse still, perhaps he knows who the murderer is. He's got to be hiding somewhere. Surely this is not going to be like Rachel's first cruise.

She determined to fill her friend in later this evening. Right now, she needed to do her job and perform the act of her life in front of Lauren.

Chapter 11

"Thank you for your patience, ladies and gentlemen, the problem is now resolved and we will start up the engines within the next ten minutes. Our course continues in a north-westerly direction towards New York and we will make up speed during the night. Please enjoy the rest of your day and take advantage of the exceptional facilities aboard the *Coral Queen*." The captain's voice reverberated throughout the ship. Rachel wondered if this unscheduled stop had involved the search for the missing crewman.

As she entered the STARS Ballroom on deck five, she saw it was crowded with a lot more people than just the Russian party. Rachel spotted Thomas clutching his trusty clipboard, ticking off names, and his face lit up when he saw her.

"Rachel, I'm pleased you decided to come. One of the ladies has gone to bed with a headache and we have a male without a dance partner. Would you mind?"

"Not at all. I'd be happy to help, seeing as you've been so kind to me, as long as it's not Nikolai," she whispered.

"No problem. He's been ordered to stay behind and do some work for Boris."

A man walked over to them. Rachel recognised him as the person who had walked slowly in front of her on the tour earlier in the day.

"Rachel... sorry, I don't know your surname?"

"Prince," she replied. "Rachel Prince."

"Rachel Prince, allow me to introduce you to Mr Asimov. Mr Asimov, Rachel will be your dance partner."

"Charmed I'm sure," he sneered, holding out his hand.

Rachel disliked the abrupt man immediately, but smiled and offered her hand. She scowled back at Thomas, but he was already dealing with the next couple on his list. Mr Asimov didn't speak as they moved on to the dance floor and his penetrating gaze made her feel uncomfortable. He clearly wasn't happy about something and made no attempt to engage in conversation.

Asimov was smaller than her at around five feet eight inches. Middle-aged and grossly overweight for his height, he had wavy shoulder-length fair hair, was clean shaven, and wouldn't have been bad looking if he'd only lose the sullen look. He wore a loud Caribbean-type short sleeved shirt with khaki knee-length shorts, the clothing completely out of synch with his dour demeanour. Through gold rimmed designer glasses, bloodshot grey eyes stared at her. *A drinker,* she mused.

"Are you enjoying your holiday so far, Mr Asimov?"

"It is satisfactory. I will be happier in New York," he replied in sharp, punctuated tones, raising his rather large nose at her, which made her want to burst out laughing.

Still no first name! This is going to be hard work.

Rachel had difficulty imagining dancing the salsa, a happy dance, with this miserable man. Thankfully, the Cruise Director arrived at that moment and took the microphone, introducing their dance instructors: a South American couple, dressed suitably for the part with bright, heavily sequined, happy clothing.

The class began with an introduction to a few basic steps where couples had to dance side by side while moving their hips rhythmically to the music. Rachel heard people laughing and having fun, but not Asimov. His moves weren't that bad, but the scowl never left his face.

"Do you like Latin dancing?" she asked.

"It's okay. I'm good, no?"

"You're good, yes," she said. "Did you enjoy the engine room tour this morning?"

"It was okay, I have background in engineering and have been on big ships in Russian navy, but I served in army."

Now we are getting somewhere. "Oh, how interesting. So how did the engine rooms compare?"

"All engine rooms alike on board ships. They may be different vessels, but they all work the same."

Pulling teeth came to mind. "Really? One thing I did notice was just how enclosed the corridors seemed, all a bit too cramped down there for me – that crew member struggled to get past us. Did you notice?"

"No, I didn't notice, I was concentrating on where we were going."

Rachel wasn't sure if he was lying, but she didn't get the chance to continue the conversation as the music stopped. The instructor paused to show them some new moves.

"Excuse me, I have to go and check how *my woman* is." Asimov spoke abruptly, turned and left.

Well I never! Rude man. Rachel moved away from the dance floor and went to join Thomas, who sat writing notes at a table to one side of the room.

"Did you realise he had the personality of a squid when you asked me to partner him? No wonder *his woman*, as he calls her, has a headache!"

Thomas laughed. "Sorry, Rachel, I didn't. I'm only just getting to grips with each of them myself. Don't you know who he is?"

"No – should I?"

"He's the oligarch. He's a billionaire and has a business empire spanning three continents, from what I can gather. I don't think any of the others like him very much – they seem frightened of him – but, according to Nikolai, he has a lot of influence in Russia."

"Blow me down with a feather! He didn't look like an oligarch – not that I have any idea what one should look like. But it doesn't excuse his blatantly rude behaviour. I never did get his first name."

"Let me see, it should be on my list – Vladimir, although he only likes to be addressed as Mr Asimov. It says here in my notes."

"There's a surprise – adds to his overinflated ego, I expect. There weren't any bodyguards with him – they seemed to be with Boris. Is he the diplomat?"

"Yes, and I find that strange, too. Those men follow Boris everywhere."

Rachel couldn't work out why this bothered her, but it did. *There's something strange going on, but I'm at a loss to know what it is.*

"Would you like to salsa with me?" asked Thomas. "I've finished for the next half an hour."

"Yes please. I must admit I enjoyed the dance, just not the partner."

"Come on then, let's hit the floor."

For the next thirty minutes, Rachel enjoyed herself. Thomas was fun to dance with, and his exaggerated salsa moves made her laugh – definitely an exhibitionist when he got going. It was not hard to imagine that with a less serious tour group, he would be a big hit. With his current group, she was sure he would have to curb his happy-go-lucky spirit somewhat.

A noticeable change of atmosphere had occurred as soon as Vladimir Asimov left, resulting in a considerably lighter mood.

The Russians let their hair down, joining in with an American party who were happily shimmying to the music, in spite of some of the men grinding rather than rotating their hips. As soon as the class ended, Thomas was surrounded by people asking what activities they had booked for the remainder of the evening.

"It seems most of them have left their itineraries in their staterooms." Thomas rolled his eyes at Rachel once the final member had left. "Thankfully I carry spares."

"They seem to be relaxing a little, though, different from this morning. Did you notice how slow the tail end of the group walked on the engineering tour?" She decided she would quiz Thomas as he didn't seem to have anything to hide – apart from being gay.

"Yes, I did. Boris got really uptight about it, but the chief engineer wouldn't slow down."

"Oh, that's interesting."

"And I overheard one of the Russians talking about your crewman. Apparently, he almost spoke to Boris, but the minders shoved him away and he scuttled off."

"Did Boris know him after all?"

"Unlikely, otherwise his minders wouldn't have been so aggressive. What slowed your end down anyway?"

"Your Mr Asimov." Her eyebrows hit the ceiling as she continued. "He decided to walk at a snail's pace about ten minutes into the tour, but then picked up the pace after that crew member passed by, funnily enough."

"Do you think there's a link? Is there something going on?"

Rachel decided she had already said and learned enough, so ended the conversation.

"I doubt it. I can't imagine an oligarch or a diplomat having anything to do with a lowly engine room worker. Anyway,

Thomas, thanks for the salsa class. I'll see you around. Can't believe we only boarded yesterday; it seems an age ago."

"It's going to seem like an eternity for me by the end of this one." He winked. "Still, I get well paid, and am hoping for a huge bonus if all goes well."

Rachel found the chief of security, Waverley, waiting outside her room when she got back.

"Chief, how nice to meet you again. I do hope you haven't found any more murderers on board since the last time I cruised."

Ignoring her quip, Waverley tightened his lips. "Miss Prince, it's a pleasure. Do you mind if I ask you a few questions?" He lowered his voice. "It's regarding your tour this morning." He coughed. Rachel had noticed on the previous cruise he had a habit of coughing when he was nervous or had something sensitive to say.

Rachel opened the door to her suite. "Please call me Rachel and do come in. Would you like a tea or coffee?"

He coughed again. "No thank you, Rachel. Sorry to intrude, but Nurse Bradshaw, erm, Sarah said that you had seen a member of the crew during your engine room tour this morning who matches the description of a man who has gone missing."

"He's still missing then?"

"Afraid so – we did stop engines for a while to scour the sea, but to be honest, there was never any likelihood of spotting him if he did go overboard. He'd been missing for some time by then. We've alerted other ships in the area, but I fear his fate is sealed if he cannot be found on board."

"Let's hope that's not the case. The man I noticed appeared frightened so might be hiding somewhere."

"Would you care to expand?"

"Well, it was the way he scurried past with his head down. His eyes were bulging and darting here and there without looking at anyone. He spoke to one of the men in the tour party in Russian, but they could have been passing the time of day for all I know. I only caught a momentary glimpse when I turned the corner of one of the corridors down near the engine room. Their tour guide said the man tried to speak to the diplomat, Boris Stanislav, but was pushed back by his minders."

"This chance encounter can have little bearing on his going missing, but if he's on board, we'll find him. There has been another unfortunate development which Sarah will fill you in on later. I understand you are meeting her this evening."

"Yes, I am, but what is it?"

"Sarah will tell you, but it must be kept completely confidential, and if I were you, I would stay out of the matter. You're a passenger and a guest while on board this ship. Not an investigator." A twinkle in his eye could have been interpreted as meaning the opposite. "Unless you want to take me up on that job offer?" He didn't wait for a reply. "Have a pleasant evening, Rachel."

Rachel was left gawping.

Chapter 12

Eager to find out what Sarah had to tell her, Rachel found time dragging, so decided to take in a show. Waverley had well and truly sucked her in, giving her half a story.

I bet it was deliberate.

He still wanted her to join his security team after having offered her a job last year and been disappointed by her refusal. A frown attached itself to her forehead, annoyed at Waverley for playing her.

With the benefit of hindsight, she wondered if it might have been better to accept his offer. Following the stabbing in Leeds, and having suffered the fallout, she had regretted her decision to return to the police force, but reason told her it would have been career suicide to leave straight after qualifying. Every new police officer needed experience.

Well, I certainly got that!

She took a seat in the main theatre and ordered a cocktail, still frowning.

The lively show provided a welcome distraction from the thoughts whirring round in her head, both past and present. The main act, a comedian, had the audience in stitches, and it felt good to laugh. She guffawed along with everyone else and, not for the first time, admired the unbelievable talent that had chosen to work on board this exemplary floating hotel.

As the resident band and dance act finished the show, she saw Thomas sitting near the front of the stage along with around twenty of his party. Tweedledee was next to Thomas and Boris, with Tweedledum squeezed into a seat on the other side of Boris. Nikolai was there next to the man who had spoken to the crewman in the morning. Tall with silver grey hair, a white beard and moustache, he wore silver-rimmed square glasses. Sitting to his right was the austere Vladimir Asimov. Next to Asimov was a woman with red hair tied up in a bun.

That must be 'his woman'. Rachel remembered how Asimov had referred to her. Deciding to move before they turned around and spotted her, Rachel headed out to make her way to the jazz bar to meet Sarah.

A crowd of people had the same idea and slowed her progress by milling around outside the entrance. Women were dressed up for the night, wearing evening gowns, and the men wore dinner suits. Trying to negotiate her way through another crowd waiting outside the public conveniences, she heard Russian voices behind her so picked up the pace. There was no point spending any more time with the arrogant Mr Asimov.

As she approached the jazz bar, she could hear ragtime music filtering out into the corridor, and when she entered, it was even more packed than it had been the previous night. Loud voices, raucous laughter along with saxophone music filled the air, and many of the passengers already looked worse for wear.

Rachel spotted Sarah at the table where they had met the night before, and Sarah waved her over. There was another woman with her who Rachel assumed must be the new nurse, Lauren, and Bernard, who she recognised from the last cruise, was there too. They were impossible to miss in their pristine white officers' uniforms, which Rachel knew was compulsory attire in public areas.

Bernard let out a wolf-whistle as Rachel approached and stood to hug her.

"Only you would do that in this day and age," scolded Sarah.

"What?" Bernard replied.

Rachel hugged him. "It's okay, Sarah, I'll let him off this once."

Bernard looked rebuked and feigned offence.

"It's a good job Brigitte isn't here otherwise he'd get one of her French lectures. I'm afraid feminism and political correctness haven't caught up with our Bernard yet."

"Well I think he's the perfect gentleman." The woman with them spoke up in a solemn tone, fracturing the light banter and mood of the moment.

"See?" said Bernard. "Someone appreciates me. This is Lauren, our new nurse. Lauren, this is Rachel, Sarah's friend."

Rachel put her hand out in greeting. "Hello, Lauren."

Lauren shook Rachel's hand, but quickly let go as if it was contaminated. *Odd girl.*

"What would you like to drink, Rachel?" asked Bernard. "I'm buying."

"Martini and lemonade – but I've got an all in drinks package so don't pay for it. Here, take my card."

Bernard walked through the crowd to the bar, and Rachel sat down. She found conversation with Lauren stilted and unnatural. The woman was at least ten years older than Sarah and Rachel, and clearly didn't want to be in their company, but she wouldn't go away. Sarah looked apologetically at Rachel, who was persevering in her attempt to make polite conversation with the American nurse.

"How are you finding life on board a cruise ship?"

"Alright."

"Have you nursed on a ship before?"

"No."

"Is it very different to working in hospitals?"

"No."

She's worse than Asimov!

Rachel gave up. Lauren's monosyllabic answers, along with the odd grunt, made her feel like she was interrogating a suspect who was taking the 'no comment' line. As soon as Bernard returned, however, Lauren's eyes lit up. Rachel couldn't help thinking this woman was immature at best, and odd at worst.

"You are more radiantly beautiful than ever, Rachel. How can that be?" Bernard continued in his usual teasing and flirtatious vein that Rachel laughed off, knowing he was happily married, but Lauren was giving her daggers.

"How's your wife?" deflected Rachel. This did the trick. Bernard was a devoted family man who loved his wife and children in Manila. He was a faithful husband who had not strayed during his three years intermittently working on cruise ships.

"She's doing very well. I have a four month break after this cruise and fly home to Manila before rejoining the ship in Australia in the New Year. Milo is five years old, Janet is three and Mikey has just had his first birthday." Bernard took out his phone and waxed lyrical over the latest photos of his children sent by his wife. He had not seen his family in almost nine months, but sent most of his salary and tips home to support their keep. Nurse pay on board a cruise ship was good, Sarah said, and he earned far more than he could earn back home. This was one of the reasons that he, and many other members of crew from poorer countries, worked away from home.

"You must be looking forward to seeing them again," Rachel said.

He wiped a tear from his eye. "More than words can say."

Sarah took his hand and gave it a squeeze, while Rachel again noted a glare that would strike down dead coming from Lauren, only this time aimed at Sarah.

"Anyway, ladies, I'm on call from 6am tomorrow, so I'm going to call it a night."

Bernard got up to leave.

"I'll walk with you, I'm tired too," said Lauren.

Bernard glanced at Sarah, pleading for help, but got a shrug of the shoulders in return. "Goodnight, you two. See you tomorrow," she said.

Rachel watched them walk away and Sarah let out a deep sigh.

"He'd better be careful," said Rachel. "She looks smitten."

"She's misunderstood his friendly demeanour to mean he's interested, but I'm sure when push comes to shove, he'll put her straight. You'd think she'd take the hint when he spoke about his wife and kids, wouldn't you?" Her tone turned grave. "Shall we go up to your suite to talk – it seems to be getting louder in here?"

"That's just what I was thinking." Rachel finished her drink, and they headed back up to deck fifteen. As Rachel was swiping the door with her card key, Mario came out of Asimov's suite, looking frazzled.

"Good evening, Miss Rachel, good evening, Nurse Sarah. Can I get you anything?"

"No thanks," replied Rachel. "We're good – I take it you've been busy this evening?"

"It has been hectic for the past hour. Mr Asimov has several guests and they conduct some business in there. Every five minutes my buzzer goes off and they order something else. First it was vodka, then it was food, and just now, more vodka. I'm hoping they are happy now – but one man is not happy. They are arguing. By the way, Miss Rachel, the tour guide you asked about, Thomas, is staying two doors down from Mr Asimov in balcony stateroom number 1508."

"Thank you, Mario. You can forget about us for the evening, but can I request a pot of coffee around 7am please?" She looked at Sarah. "I want to hit the gym early before the other passengers get moving." Sarah nodded understanding.

"No problem, miss – goodnight to you both."

Rachel and Sarah entered Rachel's suite and switched on the lights.

"I forgot how nice these suites are," remarked Sarah.

The room was delightful, Rachel had to agree. "I am lucky, aren't I? All courtesy of Queen Cruises. You should have got a free cruise too for being traumatised last year. You know, I've not seen your room. Is it the same as the one you left?"

"Yes it is, and I'm lucky that officers have their own rooms. And I'm in a balcony suite, although it has a restricted view. I have to ask you – what did you make of Lauren?"

"Well I can't say she's the friendliest person I've ever met. She seems a bit strange, but maybe she's shy."

"Agreed – I keep trying to be friendly, but she rebuffs any attempt. The only person she appears to like is Bernard, but her behaviour towards him is just weird. Maybe she'll relax when she settles in. Thankfully Gwen's a lot happier, so I suppose I'll survive either way, and hopefully we'll get Brigitte back at the end of the cruise."

"Do you know how her father is?"

"No, not yet. I'm sure she'll be in touch tomorrow."

"Okay – I can't wait any longer. Waverley said you had something to tell me." Rachel cracked open the bottle of champagne that had been waiting since yesterday. Mario had refilled the ice bucket and left out two champagne flutes, which she now filled before taking a seat next to Sarah. "Cheers. Now spill the beans."

"Cheers – I'm still digesting it myself. After I spoke with you earlier, I told Graham and Waverley about your concerns over Jefgeny in the corridor, and Waverley informed the captain. The ship stop was to do a quick search of the surrounding sea, despite the impossibility of being able to find him at that late stage if he has gone overboard."

"Yes, Waverley told me about that, and that the man is still missing."

"Well what he didn't tell you was that the captain requested Graham take another look at the body of Erik Marinov, the man who died."

Rachel's ears pricked up as Sarah explained the events of the afternoon and about the suspicious needle mark hidden in the centre of a birthmark.

"If we hadn't taken a second look, we would never have noticed it. Alex took it badly at first, but Graham has reassured him on that score. But it appears Erik's death is suspicious. No-one can be certain because sometimes crew members get hold of drugs and inject themselves, but that would be into the brachial vein, not in the upper arm. We also checked he was right-handed. The needle mark, if it is that, was in the right upper arm, meaning it had been injected by his left hand if he'd done it himself."

"The prime suspect will be his roommate then. Do they suspect Jefgeny did it?"

"They've not ruled anything out, but yes, and it might be why he's hiding – if he's hiding."

"That seems the most likely scenario, but there's still an anomaly going on within the Russian group. I'm sure that Jefgeny was frightened of someone in that group. Thomas told me he tried to speak to Boris, the diplomat, but was pushed away by his minders."

"That's odd because engineering staff have no contact with passengers and it would be inappropriate to approach them in such a way – unless he heard them speaking Russian and just forgot himself."

"Mm, that thought has crossed my mind too, and that's what Thomas seemed to make of it. There was another man in the group who spoke to Jefgeny, too. If it weren't for Jefgeny's disappearance, and now the suspicious death, I would agree with Thomas, but it all seems too much of a coincidence. You know how I hate loose ends. I take it Waverley is doing background checks?"

"You'd better believe it – he doesn't want a repeat of last year, and he's not happy with the possibility of having another murderer on board. He'd be delighted if it were Jefgeny so he could close the case. All suspicion points to Jefgeny, or another crew member who knew Erik. Waverley's ordered a search of rooms on deck C to check for drugs and needles of any kind – the crew won't be happy, but Waverley's telling them it's a spot-check, which happens occasionally. The suspicious death part is being kept quiet – even Lauren hasn't been told."

"What about the Russian party?"

"Waverley's certain they're not involved, but after last year, he trusts your instincts. On the one hand, he's saying you should stay out of it; on the other, I think he'd like you to do some informal snooping. He won't ask you, though, because he would be in trouble with the captain then, and he doesn't want to put you in any danger."

"I've already started my sleuthing. I'll join the Russians for some of their planned activities tomorrow and see if I can find out anything else."

"What are you looking for?"

"To be honest, I have no idea, but I'm hoping to recognise it when I see it. The mysterious encounter this morning might have been innocent – all I've got is a tenuous link to the Russian party."

"Please be careful, Rachel."

"I will." She raised a glass to her friend. "Cheers! Here's to us and to cruise number two, whatever it may bring."

Chapter 13

"What the hell were you thinking of, trying to speak to that man this morning?" Vladimir Asimov shouted, beside himself with rage. He was not a patient man at the best of times, but Boris Stanislav was pushing him to the limit.

"How did you find out about that?" Boris shouted back, glaring at the minders.

"I'm informed of everything, you should understand that by now."

"The man tried to speak to me – I guess he was Russian. What would you have me do – appear rude? If anything brought attention to an innocent encounter, it was *your* minders throwing their weight around. I thought they would hit him – they scared him half to death."

Vladimir stomached people like Boris frequently: social climbers who crawled their way to the top of the pile, wanting to be seen with all the right people. But he didn't trust Boris one little bit, and for that reason, he'd assigned his own personal bodyguards to keep tabs on him.

"And I suppose you didn't know the man?" Vladimir noticed beads of sweat appearing on Boris's forehead and decided to let the matter go. He needed the diplomat's co-operation – especially his ability to carry items on board in his diplomatic bags. "Let's forget about it, shall we? But please try to be a little more circumspect in the future. I have a lot at stake, and neither of us can afford for anything to go wrong. We have to remember that someone must pay your boys' school fees, and you wouldn't want your wife to find out about your little indiscretions, would you?"

"I am not trying to harm the mission; it was an innocent misunderstanding. I promise to be more careful."

Vladimir dismissed the minders for the night. "Come, Boris, let us drink vodka and forget about this little incident."

Vladimir left the bedroom where he and Boris had held this private conversation and returned to the sitting room where the others were enjoying drinks. He caught Lucretia's eye and smiled, reassuring her all was well.

The party went smoothly and Boris appeared to have gotten over his telling off. *At least he doesn't sulk*, acknowledged Vladimir, *and while I have leverage, he will do as I tell him.* The effects of the neat vodka relaxed him as it reached the back of his throat before warming his insides. Tension in his muscles dissipated. Today had been challenging. First Nikolai had pleaded with him to slow the group down because he wanted to chat up some woman – the same woman Asimov had later been forced to dance with when Lucretia developed one of her headaches. Then his minders had informed him a crewman had tried to approach Boris this morning. That must have been the crewman he'd seen passing them in the corridor – he thought he recognised the man, and wished he'd paid more attention to his face. But why did the woman, Rachel, want to know whether he'd seen the crewman?

Tension returning, his head throbbed and his neck tightened as thoughts jumbled around. Usually a calm man, he'd felt jumpy and suspicious since agreeing to do a favour for an old friend who had saved his life when they'd worked for the Russian army many years before.

Lucretia interrupted his chaotic ruminations, and he stared up into her beautiful round green eyes, her red hair now loosely wrapped around her shoulders. At thirty, in the prime of her life, she had the kind of dazzling beauty that took his breath away. Like a diamond.

"Come on, darling. You are being inhospitable. We are on holiday, let's dance."

If only you realised what was going on, he mused as he allowed her to pull him up from the sofa. Vladimir hated keeping secrets from her, but she would never allow him to do what he was going to do and would be safer if kept in the dark.

The rest of the party were enjoying themselves and classical music filled the air. He pulled her to him and they smooched before moving on to a waltz. Vladimir was a good dancer, but not as accomplished as Lucretia. He'd met her in St Petersburg when she'd played the part of Floria Tosca in the opera by Puccini and mesmerised him, both with her beauty and her voice. He'd only attended the opera reluctantly at the request of a friend who wanted to discuss a business proposition, and they'd occupied one of the best booths in the house. While his friend droned on about microchips and a new company he wanted to set up, seeking Vladimir's investment, Vladimir himself couldn't take his eyes of the woman on stage.

Later, he summoned one of his bodyguards and arranged for someone to deliver fifty red roses to the singer's room after the show, requesting an introduction. Having just come through a messy and expensive divorce, he wasn't looking for romance, but recognised from the moment he met this woman that she would hold him in the palm of her hand.

He could smell her perfume as they danced, drawing him into sublime tranquillity. When he held Lucretia in his arms, he forgot about everything except the two of them. He embraced her, comforted by the effect she had on him as it pulsated through his body.

He stopped dancing and looked into her eyes. "I love you."

The hour was late, and the others realised that their benefactor wished to be alone, so they left him with his woman.

Day 2

Chapter 14

Sarah tossed and turned all night with incessant worry about Rachel, Jefgeny and whether there was a murderer on board the *Coral Queen*. When she finally fell asleep, the sound of the telephone woke her again. On autopilot, she reached for the handset and flicked the light switch on the headboard, groggily answering, "Hello."

"Sarah, it's me." The crackly, hoarse voice was barely audible.

"Bernard?" She tried to shake herself awake, glancing at the time – 5am. "This had better be life or death. Do you realise what time it is?" she snapped.

"Sarah, it's really important. Can we meet by the pool?"

"Okay, give me fifteen minutes." She forced her weary body out of bed and took a quick shower. The nurses were woken at all hours when on call, so after her shower, she was not only awake, but alert and wondering what on earth was so important that Bernard had called her this early in the morning.

The crew pool was not visible from passenger areas, situated below and in front of the Bridge – where the captain and senior officers navigated night and day – that overhung the ship on both sides. Here, the crew got well-earned leisure time for themselves, and for many not allowed in passenger areas, it might be the only place they could breathe fresh air while at sea.

It was also where the crew let their hair down at occasional all-night parties. During these, they often called doctors and nurses to treat people who'd injured themselves falling over, or following alcohol-fuelled fighting. Senior officers turned a blind eye to most of the goings on as long as the behaviour didn't put other crew or passengers in danger. It was like any Saturday night in any big city, she had been warned when she first joined the ship.

At this time of day, all was deathly quiet, and a morning mist created an eerie backdrop to the pool. Sarah had grabbed a bacon sandwich and a flask of coffee from the crew buffet on the way. With no sign of Bernard, she sat on one of the second-hand loungers scattered around the pool. A 'Not in Use' sign explained why it was so quiet.

She finished her sandwich and was on her second cup of coffee when Bernard appeared. He looked dishevelled with dark bags under his watery eyes. Sarah had been about to scold him for being late, but seeing he was upset, she mellowed.

"What on earth's the matter?"

Tears poured down his cheeks. "I had too much to drink. Sarah, I didn't see it coming."

Sarah could imagine what he would say next even though he was struggling to speak.

"Okay, Bernard, just tell me what happened."

"On the way back to my room last night, I felt strange, unusually drunk. I'd only drunk three whiskeys – maybe I just hadn't eaten enough. I came over light headed so Lauren offered to walk me back to my room."

His eyes filled with tears again.

"Go on."

"She invited herself in and said she would help me get undressed." At this point, he started sobbing. "You can guess the rest. I woke up this morning, and she was lying there, next to me. My head is throbbing. Sarah, I have never been unfaithful to my wife. How will I be able to face her or my children again?" Tears fell down his face.

Sarah sympathised, knowing despite his jokes and flirtations, he was a one woman man – until now, that was.

He has resisted offers from crew in the past. How did this strange woman worm her way into his bed, and how will we deal with it?

"Tell me you used something?"

"I don't think so. I can't even remember what happened – that's what's so strange. I can only assume we did it as she was lying there naked."

Sarah fought the urge to laugh at his innocent use of 'did it'. "Is she still there?"

"I guess so. I called you, dressed and ran. What am I going to do?" Tear stains marked his face.

"Look, Bernard, let's be rational – it's not the first time infidelity has occurred on a cruise ship and it won't be the last.

You had too much to drink, end of story. Tell Lauren at the earliest opportunity it was a mistake and it will never happen again. Then you need to avoid spending any time alone with her for the rest of the cruise. It's not like she will be with us once Brigitte comes back."

And let's hope to God she's not pregnant! she thought.

Bernard stopped crying and Sarah gave him a hug. "Anyone who knows you knows how much you love your wife. I can't believe Lauren took advantage of your drunken state. You will get through this, and when the time is right, you can choose whether to tell your wife."

He grimaced at that part. "How did this happen? I always stay sober. I don't understand."

"I don't know how it happened, but it did. Now come on – time to get ready for work. Did you say you were on call today?"

"Yes."

"Well at least you'll be nowhere near her. I'll get her to work with me for the day, and from tomorrow, she's on her own. Are you okay going back? Do you need me to come with you?"

"I'll do it. I want to tell her as soon as possible," Bernard mumbled as he turned and headed back towards his deck, head down, broken.

Sarah's heart went out to him – he and Brigitte had been her best friends since she'd joined Queen Cruises and she would not let this strange woman ruin his life.

I should have trusted my gut. There's something rotten about that girl – Africa or no Africa.

After getting back to her room, Sarah rang Rachel to arrange to meet up for tea this afternoon, deciding not to mention the

Bernard thing at present. It wasn't her secret to tell.

On arrival at the medical centre, she spotted Lauren sitting with Graham and Gwen as bold as brass, chatting and drinking coffee.

"Sarah, good morning." Graham smiled. "I've let Alex go to get some sleep. He was up all night with a rowdy group of rugby players on holiday. They played rugby on the lido deck and one of them almost drowned! Idiots – three of them slipped and needed glueing, and one of them broke his arm rugby tackling a security officer sent to break up the party. Our security officer is no rugby player, but he's built like a battering ram."

"Oh poor boy, and poor Alex!"

"Indeed!" Gwen laughed. "Graham lets him loose on passengers rather than crew for a change, and this happens."

"Still, rather him than me! I'll do passenger surgery and you can cover crew, but call me if you need my help," said Graham, heading to the first clinic room.

"You're with me," Sarah snarled at Lauren.

"Oh, but I'm meant to be working with Bernard."

"Bernard's busy so I said I'd take you today, and tomorrow, you're working alone, with support."

Gwen looked at Sarah, shocked at her tone. Picking up something was amiss, she intervened.

"That's a superb idea, Lauren. You'll benefit from working with each member of the team so you get a feel for how we all operate. So that's settled, then."

Sarah smiled, gloating and fist-pumping in her head. *Gotcha!* Lauren glared at her, but had no choice but to follow Sarah into the clinic room.

The morning wasn't easy with a sulking assistant, but they were too busy for

Lauren to give Sarah much trouble. The brooding Lauren could do her job like a sensible professional or be difficult. Sarah didn't care either way.

After surgery, Graham had passenger visits to attend to. Sarah would have liked to accompany him herself, but she didn't want to let Lauren get away. However, she needed to check how Bernard was because he was avoiding the medical centre.

"I'm sure Lauren would enjoy shadowing you with the passengers," Sarah suggested to Graham while they were having coffee.

"Excellent idea. Come on, Lauren. Time to work with the big chief." He was in surprisingly good humour, considering the events of the day before. Lauren followed him out, scowling and shooting daggers at Sarah.

As soon as they left, Gwen turned to Sarah.

"Are you going to tell me what that was all about?"

"Would you mind if I track Bernard down first?"

"No need, here he is."

Bernard rolled in, still looking tired, but at least he was forcing a smile.

"Well?" Gwen asked.

Looking at Bernard, Sarah spoke. "We need to tell Gwen, Bernard."

Bernard slumped into a chair. "You tell her please."

Sarah related the events of last night and this morning, and Gwen listened with the occasional nod of sympathy towards Bernard. Once Sarah had finished, Gwen turned to him.

"Did you tell her it was a one-off?"

He squirmed. "I couldn't, she'd left, and this was on my bed." He handed Gwen a note.

Gwen read it out loud, "*Thank you for an amazing night – can't wait for the next time*", peered at Bernard above her spectacles and guffawed, as did Sarah, despite herself.

"An amazing night, eh? Pity you can't remember it."

"It's not funny!" Bernard sounded like a petulant child before smiling sheepishly.

"Your private life is your concern, Bernard, but if this becomes a problem, I need to know. We're too small a team to have any friction; we have to pull together. Get this resolved quickly. I will not allow an unhealthy working atmosphere. Do you understand?"

He nodded.

"Let her down gently, and then behave as if nothing happened."

Sarah wondered if that might be easier said than done.

Chapter 15

Rachel had nothing planned for today other than meeting with Sarah at three o'clock at Creams for tea. Mario brought her coffee at 7am as requested, and she had already been for a run on deck sixteen followed by forty-five minutes in the gym.

"Would you like breakfast?" Mario asked.

"No thanks, Mario, I'll eat in the buffet."

Once in the buffet, she found an empty table tucked in a corner, away from the crowds, and took out the Russian tour party's itinerary, mulling things over again. She'd had little time to speak with Sarah, but her friend had told her Jefgeny Popov was still missing and there was a growing concern for his safety. He might have killed his roommate and then thrown himself overboard later that day. Rachel had to agree that seemed the most plausible of explanations. Nevertheless, it didn't sit well with her for reasons she couldn't explain.

While she was staring at Thomas's itinerary, a familiar Jamaican voice singing in the background drew her attention. She recognised the waiter from the previous cruise as they'd often met up during her morning runs. He hadn't been there this morning, so she'd assumed he'd moved ships, but here he was at her table, large as life, smiling with a gold tooth taking pride of place instead of an upper molar.

"Good morning, ma'am. Can I get you tea or coffee?" He didn't seem to recognise her at first, and then he said, "Didn't we meet last year – I never forget a beautiful face?"

"Yes we did, on my early morning runs. I didn't see you this morning, though."

"That's right – we did. I've got a calf injury so my running days are on hold. I do weights now so I might catch you in the gym."

"Yes, I'm sure you might."

"What can I get for you on this fine morning?"

"Coffee please."

He poured her coffee and then continued to the next table, singing a few lines from *Summer Holiday* on his way. The waiter had extended his song repertoire since the last time they'd met, but he looked as skinny as ever, although more bulky around the arms and chest from his weight training. His dreadlocks had colourful braids running through them and were tied up in a ponytail.

This is what she loved about the buffet: the casual atmosphere was in stark contrast to the formality of the main restaurant where she ate her dinner each evening. Tonight was a designated formal evening where the captain and his officers met with passengers. Men would don tuxedos with a bow or black tie, while women would wear evening or cocktail dresses. Rachel appreciated the opportunity to glam up in a way she rarely experienced on land.

After a few sips of coffee, her attention returned to the itinerary in her hand. It listed many activities, including gaming lessons in the casino, sports trivia in one of the lounges, yoga, cha-cha lessons in the ballroom – which she decided to give a miss – and many others.

Rachel chose a wine tasting lesson at midday, thinking she might learn something. She had no clear plan, but the itinerary helped pass the time during sea days, and she liked Thomas. She hoped there wouldn't be anything to discover and the matter of Jefgeny and Erik would be a neat, albeit tragic, murder/suicide. This would be preferable to a murderer running loose on the ship – again.

Staff had cordoned a small area of the wine bar off for the wine tasting lesson. Thomas stood in the centre, armed with his usual clipboard, and beamed.

"Rachel, it's great you came. Please stay with me." He nodded her a warning towards Nikolai, knowing she wasn't keen.

Boris and his macho minders, Tweedledee and Tweedledum, sat at one of the tables, along with Nikolai and Vladimir Asimov, *his woman* hanging on to his arm. Rachel admired the woman's sultry beauty, hour-glass figure and gorgeous long red hair, which was flowing down her back while enhancing her porcelain-like facial features. The woman looked her way and smiled.

Embarrassed at being caught staring, Rachel smiled back, and then turned her attention back to Thomas.

"I'm looking forward to this lesson, being a wine lover who doesn't understand what I'm supposed to be looking for when I'm poured a sample in a restaurant."

"I'm a scotch man myself, but I like a glass of wine too, and yes, this is one of the more useful sessions. Beats origami!"

Rachel chuckled and took a seat next to Thomas, then looked around, listening in to any conversations held in English. Nikolai looked agitated and stuck like glue to Boris today, whispering in his ear as soon as Asimov moved. They sat two tables ahead of her so she couldn't make out the words.

"Mr Asimov seems a lot happier today," Rachel whispered to Thomas.

"He seems much more relaxed when Lucretia is with him. He's the perfect gentleman then," Thomas acknowledged.

"Neither is wearing a wedding ring, so I assume they're not married?"

"No, I heard one of the others saying he had not long since come through a messy divorce that cost him a vast amount of his considerable wealth when they met. I don't think it will be long, though, he seems besotted."

"Well I grudgingly admit he seems to be a different person today."

"She is rather beautiful – a man could go straight looking at you two." Laughing out loud, causing a few heads to turn their way, Rachel thumped him on the arm. To anyone watching, it would appear they were striking up an early romance, and Rachel played along.

After the wine tasting session, she mingled. The ones she particularly wanted to get a handle on included Boris,

Asimov, and the man who'd appeared to be speaking to Jefgeny the day before, but he wasn't there.

Rachel walked over to Boris, watched by the Tweedle twins. Grinning at her inner joke and ignoring them, she spoke to Boris.

"Thank you for allowing me to gatecrash some of your activities."

Boris looked a little bit uncomfortable, almost fearful as he looked at the short, stocky minder, Tweedledee. "It is no trouble at all. There is always one of the group who ends up not coming."

"Nevertheless, I'm grateful. May I buy you a glass of that exquisite wine we just sampled?" Rachel hoped he wouldn't get the wrong impression, but saw his wedding ring and assumed it would be okay. "Is your wife here? Perhaps I can buy her a drink too?"

"No, she is not here. They base us in America, but I am taking this cruise to conduct some business. When the ship returns to Southampton, we will continue on to the Baltic where the group will leave ship and I will fly back to New York from Russia." He still looked nervous and kept looking at his minders.

"In that case, it's just you and me, and as I owe Thomas a drink, I'm sure he'll join us." Then she looked at the Tweedle twins. "I'm sure these gentlemen can keep an eye on you from a distance."

The minders nodded and moved away, resulting in a more relaxed Boris. Rachel called Thomas over, and after buying drinks, found a booth away from prying ears.

"It must be so interesting being a diplomat. Do you like America?"

"It's alright. I haven't been stationed there long. Before I lived in Paris; I like France very much."

"Did you have to move?"

"Mother Russia decides where we should be." He spat out the words and she exchanged a cursory glance with Thomas, surprised at the venom in Boris's tone. As if sensing he had spoken out of turn and looking around, he continued. "Don't get me wrong, I love my country; it's just that my family had settled in France and my wife and I had to leave our two sons behind as they'd started university. My wife misses them and it makes life difficult."

"Paris is beautiful," said Thomas. "I've led many tours through the sights of that wonderful city. But I'm sure you and your wife will grow to love New York – there is so much to do there."

"How long have you known Mr Asimov?" Rachel wanted to move the conversation along, sensing Boris becoming morose.

Boris's face reddened. "Not long. We have business to conduct, that is all."

Now that reaction is interesting, thought Rachel, sensing the animosity and confirming her first impressions of Asimov.

Rachel saw Asimov speaking harshly to the Tweedle twins, who were now heading towards their table. Tweedledee spoke.

"Mr Asimov wants to continue with meeting now."

"Oh let the man finish his drink," said Thomas, but the minders were unmoved.

"I had better go. Thank you for the drink, Rachel. We will no doubt see you again at some of our other activities." He rose to leave, shaking Thomas's hand before the minders flanked him either side.

"That's an odd way to protect someone," said Thomas. "Normally the one being protected is in charge, but in that relationship, it seems to be the other way around."

"Yes, I had the same thought," remarked Rachel. She needed to find out more about that, but for now she felt hungry.

"You've hardly touched your wine, Rachel."

"I know, I don't drink that much. Not sure why I bought it. I think I'll get lunch now. Where are you heading next?"

"I'm lunching with ten of the group in the main restaurant. Tonight I'm accompanying Mr Asimov, Lucretia, Boris, Nikolai and three other ladies for dinner at the captain's table after the formal evening events are over."

"Impressive," she answered. "See you again soon."

Rachel rose from the booth seat, noting a suggestion that Waverley might want to get a seat at the captain's table. With luck, he might even wangle Rachel and Sarah in too.

She passed through the main atrium on her way to lunch and watched chefs creating the enormous ice sculptures they would display during the evening. There was a magnificent sculpture of the Empire State Building and an extensive array of other American themed creations, but the one that impressed her the most was the multi-coloured American flag with a ripple effect that made it appear to be blowing in the wind. Red, white and blue ice flowed through it to make it even more realistic, fifty stars representing the number of states in America. It was unsurpassed.

Rachel ate a light lunch in the buffet before heading down to the lido deck, and then walked around the ship for a while, thinking about what little she had discovered so far. A murder had been committed on board the ship and the chief suspect, Jefgeny Popov, was now missing, presumed dead. Some interaction had taken place between the missing man and at least two members of the Russian group. Did this have a bearing on his going missing soon afterwards? She thought it unlikely; he was probably on his way into hiding or suicide when she saw him in the corridor, otherwise he would have been at work in the engine room. That would rule out the Russians being part of a conspiracy.

What of Boris's reaction today? He obviously didn't like being part of this group and appeared to be guarded rather than minded. Why would that be? Her gut told her something was amiss, and after the events of the last cruise, she wouldn't be dissuaded from following the investigation through. She would try to get Waverley to agree to the next stage and see where it led.

She looked at her watch – time to meet up with Sarah.

Chapter 16

Sarah stayed with Bernard after morning surgery, in spite of being off duty. She wanted to make sure he was alright, so she attended a few on-board passenger injuries with him. He brightened up a little as the hours wore on and managed to banter with injured passengers in his usual way.

An elderly man had sprained his wrist while trying out the golf simulator. "I think I put a bit too much wrist into my swing," he explained.

"Perhaps you should save your strength for lifting cocktails," Bernard joked, and they immediately hit it off. As Bernard engaged with passengers and crew like his normal self, it seemed to be helping him forget the trauma of his shock awakening. Sarah would be glad once he'd managed to speak with Lauren and clear the air. Sadly, it wouldn't undo the faux pas of the previous night, and she worried about how he would live with that.

Gwen had called a team meeting for 1pm and Raggie, the medical team steward, would bring lunch up from the kitchen. Bernard and Sarah headed back down to the medical centre. The arrogant Lauren was already there, along with Graham and Alex. Gwen sat at her desk, while Raggie brought in extra chairs so that they could all sit down.

Gwen kicked the meeting off. "I thought it would be prudent to have a proper meeting as Sarah has now rejoined us and we've got a new team member, Lauren Blythe."

Bernard kept his head down, staring at the floor.

"We also have a number of passengers with long-term conditions, and as it's only our second sea day, Graham would like to update us on a few of these. I will let him go first, and then he and Alex can carry on with their work while we have a nurse meeting afterwards."

"Thank you, Gwen," Graham began. "There are five passengers I would like you to know about in case they call, and there are some I should warn you about, but I'm sure you will suss those out for yourselves!" He laughed. "Lauren, you're new to the ship so it's important that you learn and follow ship procedure at all times. If there is anything that you don't understand, I'm sure that Sister Sumner – Gwen – has already told you to ask. We are all very approachable, but there is a hierarchy on board a cruise ship that you may not be used to."

Sarah thought Graham sounded niggled about something and wondered if Gwen had filled him in on the Bernard situation, but doubted it. Nevertheless, something had rattled him. She felt curious as to whether she had missed something, but was pretty certain she had been listening. She paid double attention now.

"Of course," Lauren replied, sullenly.

Graham continued. "We have a seventy year old lady in 7160 with chronic obstructive pulmonary disease who carries portable oxygen when out and about on the ship. An oxygen concentrator was delivered to her room on embarkation day." He turned to Lauren again. "Are you familiar with concentrators?"

"They don't have them in the depths of Africa."

Missing or choosing to ignore the sarcasm, Graham explained. "Oxygen concentrators are big beasts, about the size of a large portable air conditioning unit – they convert room air to concentrated oxygen. She uses nasal specula rather than a mask so that she can carry on as normal without constantly removing the mask. You will only need to see her if she develops a chest infection while you are on call or if anything goes wrong with the equipment. Call me if in doubt – understood?"

"Understood," they replied in unison. The problems associated with a transatlantic crossing boiled down to the number of sea days if equipment broke down. They carried one concentrator and oxygen cylinders in the infirmary for emergencies.

"We also have a gentleman with lung cancer who's joined us for what he says will be his final cruise, having been given only a few months to live. Gwen and I have met with him and we will continue to take the lead in his care, so call us if needed. I just hope the poor man survives the journey – he's not in the best of health and I wonder if he fabricated the amount of time he has left when completing his medical questionnaire. However, it is what it is, and we will do our best.

"There's a teenager with a broken leg – broke it playing football a few days before the cruise. He's in plaster and may need one of you if the plaster needs replacing – he's a low risk for thrombosis, but be on the lookout, just in case. One of the Russians, a Mr Sergei Markov, is diabetic and hasn't brought enough insulin with him. He swears he did and it's gone missing, but he only has a third of a bottle with him, so will need fresh supplies – I'll leave that with you.

"Finally, another one of the Russians takes regular morphine tablets for chronic back pain. I've explained to him the importance of keeping supplies locked in his stateroom." Graham got up from his chair. "Well that's it from me. There are other passengers with medical conditions that are all on the computer if you get called out, but I thought I'd let you know about these five. I'll see you this evening, then."

Graham left the room.

"Do you have anything to report, Alex?" asked Gwen.

"No, most of the crew are in good health. Obviously they would be in better health if they didn't drink quite so much, but what can I say? Christine, the perfume shop manager, is five and a half months pregnant, but there are no complications at present. She will leave us on our return to England. There's the missing man who needs blood tests if he turns up, but that doesn't seem likely."

Alex got up and left the office. Neither of the medics had mentioned the late Erik Marinov.

Gwen continued the nurses' part of the meeting, explaining to Lauren what would be expected of her from tomorrow. Sarah was pleased Lauren would no longer be shadowing either her or Bernard, thinking it might be easier to work with her from a distance.

At the end of the meeting, Gwen turned to Bernard.

"Bernard, please show Lauren where the insulin is and how to sign it out so she can take a supply up to Mr Markov." She gave him a look of encouragement as he left with the enthusiastic Lauren trailing behind like a puppy dog.

"That should be that. He has the opportunity to bring an end to this awkward situation." Gwen exhaled a deep breath as if remembering something. Sarah felt guilty about knowing Gwen's secret. "I expect Bernard told you about an unfortunate relationship on my previous ship, and although different to this mishap – the eventual outcome amounted to the same thing. I just hope this girl takes no for an answer. Difficult relationships in the confined space where we all live and work together are not at all pleasant. I'm relying on you, Sarah, to do your best to get on with Lauren in spite of your friendship with Bernard. We can't have factions."

"I'll try, but she hasn't responded to 'friendly' yet."

Gwen groaned. "Well let's give it a go and see how it plays out. At least it's only for a fortnight. I've never seen Bernard drunk so don't understand how he managed to get into such a compromising state."

Sarah had to admit this had bothered her too. She'd worked with Bernard for nine months prior to her leave and he'd always remained in control of his faculties. For a start, medical staff could be called upon to assist even when not on call, so she didn't get it. Maybe he'd just let his guard down.

Gwen shuffled, waiting for a reply, staring at her, nonplussed.

"Sorry, I was miles away. I don't get it either, but I'm certain it will never happen again. I'd better go; I'm meeting Rachel for tea."

She omitted to say that Rachel was doing some sleuthing among the Russian contingent.

On her way out of the medical centre, Sarah almost crashed into Waverley. Then Lauren barged past her.

"See you later," Sarah called, but got no reply.

Waverley looked bemused. "Is something wrong?"

"No, I don't think so."

"Anyway, you're just the person. I wanted to have a word with you and your friend."

"I'm on my way to meet her for tea," Sarah replied.

"Could you both drop by my office afterwards? I'm sure she won't keep herself out of our little mystery so we may as well compare notes." He frowned, but couldn't hide a smirk. "Your friend does seem to have a dog with a bone attitude."

"Yes, it was the same at school. Rachel always uncovered wrong-doing. She put an end to a pocket money thieving racket by hiding out in the girls' loos and filming the gang bragging about it. They targeted weak kids and threatened them. She's always championed the underdog and detests bullies. I'm not surprised she's ended up in the police force."

"Well, well, well." Waverly stroked his chin.

"Anyway, we'll be there in an hour," said Sarah before dashing off to change from her blue scrubs into a white uniform for the passenger decks.

Bernard came out of the medicine room and saw that Sarah had already left. Gwen called him into her office, pleased to see him smiling.

"I take it your smile means it went well," she said.

"Not really, she's very angry and says it's all my fault that she has fallen for me – she says I led her on. I did try to explain that my flirting is just my way, and it means nothing."

"I expect that went down like a lead balloon!"

"How did you know? Yes, it seemed to make her angrier, and she gave me a ticking off."

"So why are you smiling?"

"Oh," he beamed, "that's because she says nothing happened. She said I passed out and that she got into bed with me, hoping that it would happen this morning, but when she woke up, I was gone."

Gwen sniggered, feeling pleased for Bernard. "At least there's no real harm done. Well, let that be a lesson to you – cut out the flirting."

"Don't worry, I've learned my lesson, and she's already told me I'm a huge disappointment to her, so thankfully she won't be renewing her affections. I can't wait to tell Sarah that I am still a faithful married man."

At that point, his on-call radio signalled he was needed elsewhere.

"Go on, off with you." Gwen couldn't help chuckling again, pleased that a potentially sticky situation had been averted with the minimum of fuss. She was finally starting to feel happy after the heartbreak of her own relationship.

If only nothing had happened there, she thought as she remembered the heart wrenching pain she'd experienced when transferring away from the only man she'd ever loved. Exhaling loudly, she turned towards the computer to create invoices for medical treatments administered this morning.

Chapter 17

Rachel made her way down to Creams patisserie and arrived at exactly the same time as Sarah.

"I can't get over how lovely you are in your shiny white uniform."

"You don't look so bad yourself," Sarah replied. They hugged and walked into the small café together. There was a surcharge on food and drinks in Creams so it was quieter than many of the public eating areas. They sat down and ordered tea while looking at the menu.

"Are you going to eat?" Rachel asked.

"I'll have something sweet. We had a working lunch during a team meeting."

The waiter came over to take their orders.

"I'll have a strawberry cheesecake, please, and tea," said Sarah.

"Chocolate cake for me and filter coffee, please," added Rachel.

As soon as the waiter had gone, the young women nattered about their day for a while and laughed a lot, something they always did when they were together. Once the food had arrived, and they were left to themselves, Rachel was keen to ask if there had been any developments in the case she was now informally investigating.

"Nothing further our end. Jefgeny is still missing. I bumped into Waverley on the way to meet you. He's acknowledged that you'll be looking into the Russians and wants us to stop by his office after tea for an information exchange."

"Oh, that sounds interesting. I wonder if he has anything meaty to share. I'm not getting very far with the Russians, but I'll share what I've discovered. Shall we do it all afterwards, then?"

"Yes, I'd far rather talk about trivia at the moment. It's been quite a day."

Rachel sensed Sarah had something on her mind, but knew that if her friend wanted to share it, she would. *It's probably something confidential to do with her work.*

"Okay, trivia it is. I went to a wine tasting lesson today and discovered many things I never knew before, ignoramus that I am!"

"Come on, then, spill the beans – I thought you looked blurry eyed."

Rachel laughed out loud. "The wine they got us to taste was pretty strong, and then I had a part-glass with Thomas and Boris afterwards – trying to get to know Boris, but our drink was short lived when the minders butted in. I'm not very good at lunchtime drinking."

"There's so much booze available on the ship, but officers have to watch the amount they drink, and our team has to be careful even when off duty as you never know when the next major emergency might occur."

"This chocolate cake is scrummy," said Rachel as she took a big bite.

They spent the next hour discussing wine tasting and chocolate before Sarah looked at her watch.

"I guess we should go see Waverley. I need to get back to the medical centre for early evening surgery afterwards, and then change into yet another uniform for formal night."

The ship enforced an ultra-strict uniform policy for staff, and those allowed in the passenger areas wore different uniforms for different occasions. Sarah had told her previously that about a third of the crew never got to be in passenger areas at all. There were even different tiers of eating for those considered staff and those considered crew.

"Okay," Rachel replied. "And on the way, you can remind me about who eats where."

Before they left, Sarah signed the chit for payment. Rachel also signed as all her food and drink was free, courtesy of Queen Cruises.

They arrived at an office on deck three with a shiny bronze plaque on the door that read 'Security Office'. Sarah knocked and entered. Rachel followed and noted how pristine it was, like everything else on the *Coral Queen*. There was a monstrous oak desk with a veneer so shiny Rachel could see her reflection.

Chief Security Officer Waverly was seated on a large black leather office chair which swivelled away from them while he spoke on the telephone. He acknowledged them with his hand, without looking, motioning for them to take a seat. There was a small settee on one side of the room and two comfy chairs with a round glass table at the centre. There was also a fixed chair opposite the large desk.

Sarah opted for the settee and Rachel joined her, realising that in spite of her dealings with Waverley on the previous cruise, she had never been inside his office. Sarah smiled at her and they waited for the chief to finish his telephone conversation.

As soon as he put the telephone down, he swivelled his chair back towards them and rose.

"Sorry about that. Can I get either of you ladies a drink?" He moved towards them and took one of the seats.

"No thank you, we're good," Sarah answered for both of them.

Rachel felt like she was sitting in the headmaster's office at school waiting for Waverley to get to the point.

He looks tired, she thought, *it can't be easy trying to investigate a murder on board a cruise ship while also being responsible for the safety of over six thousand people and answerable to the captain on all matters of security.*

"I'll get straight to the point. First of all, Rachel – I realise you're not a member of the security team and you ought not to be involved in this investigation at all. The only reason you are here is because experience tells me you won't keep out of it."

He smiled grimly.

"I have been doing some background checks on our Russian crew members, Erik Marinov and Jefgeny Popov. First, Marinov had no criminal record. His background was clean, and he was a model employee for three years – no girlfriends; no fallouts with his friends who, incidentally, speak highly of him. We can find no motive for anyone to want to kill him, except perhaps his roommate."

He paused, allowing this information to sink in.

"Now to Mr Popov. He's also unmarried, brought up in the USA and a US citizen. He has a background in engineering and both parents are dead – other than that his background is a bit sketchy, but nothing pointing towards being a killer."

"If he was brought up in the USA, why couldn't he speak English?" asked Sarah. "When I saw him on embarkation day, he used Erik as an interpreter."

"That is odd. I don't know, but I'll certainly find out. Perhaps he was playing a joke on you."

"Is it possible the two men were in a relationship?" asked Rachel.

"I wondered that, but Mr Popov has a girlfriend on board. She is Slovenian and works in the casino. She is obviously distraught at his disappearance, but says she hasn't seen him since yesterday morning. I haven't told her his roommate may have been murdered; she insists they were good friends and confirms what others have said: that Erik took Jefgeny under his wing ever since he joined the ship two years ago. By all accounts, they got on well, and all eight Russians working in engineering corroborate this. All the others are clean. I had expected nothing else, to be honest – our pre employment checks are rigorous."

Waverley didn't hide his defensiveness at this point. It was clear he had hoped the murder would have been a falling out between the two crew members that ended with the death of Erik Marinov.

"What about the girlfriend?" Rachel enquired.

"Eva Sipka – she has a clean record. No-one with a criminal record may work in the casino. She and Jefgeny have been seeing each other for the past six months and are in a steady relationship. It also turns out Miss Sipka might be pregnant; she's not yet had this confirmed by the medical team, but I have insisted she make an appointment to see Dr Romano for a pregnancy test and examination. As you can imagine, this has caused her even more distress."

"Oh my goodness!" gasped Sarah. "That's just what a girl needs – a partner who goes missing and a baby on the way."

"Welcome back to the *Coral Queen*." Waverley grimaced.

"Can I see a picture of the girlfriend?" Rachel asked.

Waverley walked over to his desk, fired up his computer and pulled up the record.

"Here you go, take a peek."

Rachel and Sarah both looked at the image of a woman in her twenties with dyed blonde hair. She had green eyes and her face was thin with pronounced cheek bones.

"Thank you," Rachel said and returned to the settee.

"There is something else." Waverley's tone turned more serious.

"What?" asked Rachel, noticing that he appeared unsure of whether to give them any additional information.

"Someone ransacked Jefgeny's room last night. It's difficult to say whether the person or persons were looking for something or were opportunistic thieves. Both scenarios create problems for security. We have sealed off the room and changed the swipe code."

"Was anything taken?"

"They took a watch and a radio, but we don't know what else was there. We didn't find his passport when we searched the room yesterday and we have not touched the room since."

"What about CCTV?" asked Sarah.

"We don't monitor the crew passageways. The crew need to let their hair down sometimes."

He coughed and looked down at his shoes.

"Now we move on to the Russian party, although I can't see how they can be involved in this matter at all." He sounded frustrated. "But, I failed to follow your gut instinct last year, Rachel, and I do not want to make the same mistake. You understand I'm being over-cautious."

Rachel understood his frustration, certain that Asimov and Boris would have no qualms about making life difficult if they imagined for a moment they were under any kind of investigation.

Waverley continued. "There are thirty two members in the group, twenty-one men and eleven women. Eight of the women are clean, with one of those being a renowned international opera singer, a Miss Lucretia Romanov. I saw her myself in Verdi's *La Traviata* a few years ago in St Petersburg." Waverley blushed at the reminiscence.

"That's Asimov's girlfriend," said Rachel.

Waverley coughed before continuing. "Anyway, two of the women have been fined for prostitution in the past, and one faced an assault charge after attacking her ex-husband's lover with a cricket bat."

"Nice," remarked Sarah.

"They released her after the victim dropped charges." Waverley coughed as per his habit, so Rachel guessed that something interesting was coming next. "Now for the men – it has not been easy to get much information about Vladimir Asimov, other than that he is a very rich man – self-made billionaire with a large empire. He is an ex-soldier who served in the Russian army during the cold war and had friends in the KGB. There have been rumours of links to industrial espionage, but nothing proven. There are also rumours his accusers tend to disappear, but as I say, these are rumours, and Russia sometimes thrives on disinformation and fake news.

"I have an old friend who is also ex soviet army. He now works for the Russian police force. He will make some discreet enquiries for me, but has to be careful not to end up in trouble. Asimov is a powerful man in Russia. Anyway, I believe none of this has anything to do with our murder and is unlikely to be relevant.

"The other person of interest is Nikolai Stepanov."

At this point, Rachel sat up straight – he would definitely be on her list of suspects.

"Interesting," she said. "He appears to be a bit cloak and dagger."

"As well he might be," Waverley continued. "He's well educated – studied at Yale University where he did a degree in engineering."

"That gives us an engineering link," Rachel pointed out.

"Probably coincidence – anyway, he served in the Russian Navy as a chief engineer and is also rumoured to have links with organised crime. He works as personal assistant to Boris Stanislav, diplomat. We cannot find much background on Boris, other than that he's married, has two sons and works at the Russian embassy in New York. He has diplomatic immunity, but there are no rumours surrounding him. I've asked my Russian friend to dig up anything relevant in his background. The rest of the men have clean background checks and appear to be legitimate businessmen."

"What about the bodyguards?" Rachel asked.

"I have run their names and they are both ex-soldiers who boxed during their army days and provide personal security to Vladimir Asimov. What makes you think they are Boris's bodyguards?"

"Now that is interesting," said Rachel. "They are minding Boris, but I got the distinct impression he wasn't their boss and was happy to get away from them. I'm sure there's more to this setup, but whether it has anything to do with the crime on board this ship is another matter."

"Well, we don't want to get involved in any personal Russian business problems," said Waverley. A worried frown appeared on his face.

"All I've found out so far is that Boris does not seem happy. I suspect he's being guarded rather than protected, and you've just confirmed that." Rachel looked at Waverley and then continued. "I don't like Nikolai, but that doesn't mean he's up to no good. Asimov appears moody and must have assigned his own security to Boris for some reason. Mario said the Russians were arguing the other night, but I thought nothing of it at the time. There might be some unrelated shady business dealings. Nothing links any of them to the murdered crewman, or to the missing Jefgeny – so far." Exasperated, she added, "And who is the tall, thin man who said something to Jefgeny when we were on our tour of the engine room?"

Waverley got up again and moved across to his computer, pulling up images of all the Russian party for Rachel.

"That's him," she said as he scrolled through the photos.

"Let me see – he is Sergei Markov, also an engineer and also at Yale around the same time as Nikolai. He started a year earlier. He is fifty-three years old with a wife in Moscow, listed as next of kin – she does not appear to be on this cruise." Waverley ran his hands through his thinning hair. "We have to keep this in perspective – if we ran checks on all our tour groups and passengers, we would find something dodgy, so what we urgently need to do is find out what has happened to Jefgeny Popov."

"True enough," agreed Rachel.

"Sorry, but I need to get back to the medical centre," said Sarah.

"Yes, and I need to dress for the formal evening," said Rachel. "Is there anything else?" she asked Waverley.

"Yes, just stay out of trouble, and *do not* stir up a hornets' nest with the Russians unless there's anything relevant. My hunch is this is a murder/suicide for reasons we cannot yet explain."

"Guides' honour." Rachel smiled as she left Waverley's office, knowing exactly where she was going to sleuth next.

Chapter 18

Rachel studied her outfit in the mirror before leaving her suite. It had taken ages to decide what to wear to the formal evening. Most women would be wearing elegant full-length evening dresses with matching stole. That would have been her first choice, except she wanted to hide away in the sports bar next to the casino once the captain and his officers had finished their introductions.

Eventually, she opted for a royal-blue cocktail dress, appropriate for the evening, but not too dressy for the sports bar. The creative use of curling tongs produced soft waves through her hair. Satisfied with the result, she applied a light smattering of makeup and smiled at herself in the mirror, wishing Carlos was here to compliment her.

Rachel looked forward to seeing the men in their tuxedos, although none could look more striking than Carlos in a tux. A pang of guilt made her shudder, knowing he would be worried sick if there was any mention of the murder.

Mario passed her in the corridor. "Good evening, Miss Rachel, may I say you look radiant this evening?"

"Thank you, Mario. I see you're busy as usual." He had his hands full, carrying a tray towards Asimov's room.

"Yes, ma'am. Pre-dinner drinks for the men. They having dinner with the captain so are not worried about attending the formalities until later."

"Oh yes, Thomas told me earlier."

Blast – she had forgotten to mention it to Waverley during their meeting. *Oh well, I don't expect it would have revealed much anyway,* she reassured herself.

"If you pick up any mention of a crewman from engineering, would you let me know?"

Mario looked concerned. "I hope you're steering clear of danger, Miss Rachel."

"Of course I am, Mario. They might know someone I met, that's all, and I don't want to appear nosey or I'd ask them myself."

The explanation didn't convince her, let alone Mario, but he nodded anyway.

"Goodnight, see you in the morning." Rachel walked towards the lifts and stairwell, deciding to take the stairs, even in high heels.

The main atrium was packed with dazzlingly dressed women. The men looked dapper in their smart well-pressed suits. A waiter offered her champagne, and she took a flute from his tray and helped herself to canapés. Thomas waved from across the room, gesturing he would come over to her. She laughed as he struggled through the crowds of people, who were excited to meet the captain for the first time. Formal evenings were a highlight of the cruise calendar for many passengers.

The captain stood, patiently shaking hands, having photos and selfies taken with as many people as he could before making his way towards the ice carvings where he would introduce the senior officers one by one. Rachel had met Captain Peter Jensen on the previous cruise and he spotted her as he passed by. "Miss Prince, it's good to meet you again. I heard you were aboard." Being surrounded by passengers, he omitted to mention any trouble afoot. To look at him, you wouldn't imagine he had a care in the world.

Just what you need in a ship captain, she told herself.

"Good evening, Captain. It's a pleasure to be on the *Coral Queen* again."

"Captain, this way—" Voices called for his attention from every direction and he obliged the more excitable guests who wanted to shake his hand.

Thomas appeared. "This is like being at a pop concert," he said as he made his way over to her. "But no drugs! You look stunning this evening. You're always beautiful, but tonight you have excelled yourself."

"Hello, Thomas. You're rather dashing yourself. You do scrub up well – a tuxedo suits you. Is that Armani?"

"Yes – one of the perks of being single is I can splash out on expensive clothing. Isn't it exciting, seeing the captain?" Thomas glowed at the prospect of meeting Captain Jenson. Rachel smiled, not wanting to brag.

"Yes, it is one of the most surreal parts of cruising. Where are your charges?"

"Oh, most of them are around here somewhere." He waved his arms in the general direction of where he'd come from. "Mr Asimov and Boris are joining us soon, and then we'll meet the captain for dinner. I'm buzzing. I hope I'll be able to eat without dropping anything in my lap or spilling a drink."

"You'll be your normal, efficient self, I'm sure," she said, reassuringly. "Does that mean Boris gets rid of his minders for a few hours?"

"Yes, he does. In fact, he's told them to stay away from him. He and Mr Asimov had a heated debate about it. They forget sometimes I'm fluent in Russian."

Rachel's ears pricked up, and she grabbed two more glasses of champagne from a passing waiter's tray – handing one to Thomas.

"Tell me more," she whispered, conspiratorially.

"Well, I was waiting in Mr Asimov's suite for him to confirm arrangements for the evening when Boris barged in. He completely ignored me and marched towards Mr Asimov. 'Call them off, Vladimir, or the deal's off,' he shouted at him. 'I mean it – I'm fed up with them throwing their weight around. I can't breathe with them around all the time, so make it happen.' Mr Asimov shrugged his shoulders, saying he would deal with it. He then turned back to me, cool as you like, and told me in English to go through the evening's arrangements. It's because they speak such good English they forget about my Russian."

"I can't blame Boris for wanting space," said Rachel, thoughtfully. This confirmed what she had suspected: Asimov was having Boris watched, but what deal was Boris referring to, and did it have any relevance to the missing crewman?

The microphone burst into life, interrupting Rachel's thoughts, and the cruise director welcomed everyone before introducing the captain.

"Ladies and gentlemen, I give you – Captain Jensen." Loud applause followed the announcement, and the captain took over the microphone.

"Thank you all, and again, I welcome you aboard the magnificent *Coral Queen*. First, I would like to draw your attention to the wonderful ice carvings created by our own world-renowned chefs. They depict the state of New York and the American flag. We will dock in New York in five days' time, but in the meantime, there is plenty for you to enjoy aboard this magnificent vessel."

More applause followed, and Captain Jenson provided a brief history of his maritime experience before starting his introductions.

"Now I would like to introduce to you the finest senior officers I have had the pleasure to sail with." Further applause followed, and the captain introduced each of his senior officers, including the familiar CSO Waverley, the chief engineer, Steven Rafferty, and Dr Graham Bentley, CMO. There was a senior officer for everything, from housekeeping and hospitality services right up to the deputy captain.

Sarah wasn't there, and Rachel assumed she was busy in the medical centre. Alex stood with a group of other officers, and Lauren stood close to a few of the Russians Rachel recognised, including Sergei Markov, whom she had yet to speak to. She decided to ask Thomas to introduce her, but would need to invent an excuse for him to do so without arousing suspicion. It could wait because she had other plans for this evening.

As the captain finished, Rachel observed Dr Bentley being hurried away, followed by Boris, and then Thomas's radio came to life. He looked concerned as he listened to the message and paled before her.

"What is it?" she asked as he put the radio away.

"It's Nikolai. Someone has found him dead in his room. The doctor's on his way. I need to go – this is a terrible turn up."

He turned away and headed towards the lift. Rachel followed.

"Wait, Thomas! I'm coming with you – you might need support."

He smiled appreciatively and slowed down. "I'd be grateful. Let's take the elevator – nothing like this has happened before. I'm not sure what I'm meant to do."

The lift was full of other passengers, so they spoke no more. Thomas was almost in tears – she wasn't sure what state he would be in when they arrived.

As soon as they got to deck fifteen, Rachel caught sight of Sarah, Graham, Alex and Bernard heading briskly towards them and the lifts with a stretcher. She assumed Nikolai's body was being transported down to the morgue.

"Make way, please," Dr Bentley called out to curious bystanders gathering in the corridor as the stretcher rushed past. Rachel recognised an IV bag being held in the air by Sarah as they raced towards the lift and realised what was happening.

"He's not dead." She gripped Thomas's arm, seeing he looked like he might pass out, and mouthed to Sarah that she would follow her down later. "Come on, Thomas. We need to find out what happened. Let the medical team do their job."

Rachel frog-marched Thomas towards a crowd of Russians gathered outside the stateroom she assumed belonged to Nikolai.

"Miss Prince, what brings you here?" Vladimir looked unhappy.

"I was with Thomas when he got the urgent call and came to ask if there is anything I can do."

"As you see, it seems to be under control. Mr Stepanov has taken ill, and the doctors have taken him to the infirmary."

A distraught voice sobbed out, "Taken ill? I thought he was dead."

Rachel noticed an elegantly dressed long-haired brunette sitting on a chair inside the stateroom, being comforted by two other women, one of whom was Asimov's *woman,* the famous opera singer.

Rachel took the opportunity to follow Thomas into the room. He walked towards the hysterical woman and took her hand, having regained control of himself, so Rachel could take in the scene before her.

The room was littered with miscellaneous empty wrappers tossed on the floor, left behind by the medical staff. Nikolai's suit hung over a chair where he had seemingly placed it neatly to dress for the evening. His shirt lay on the floor. She picked it up and noticed someone had cut it in half.

"The doctor cut it." The crying woman sounded more coherent. "They needed to put drip up. They got ready to do CPR."

Rachel nodded and put the shirt on the chair, noticing as she did so a pill bottle under the bed, which she picked up.

"I'll call down to the medical centre and ask how he is," she said.

"You can use phone in our room," Asimov's girlfriend said.

Rachel slipped the pill bottle into her clutch bag and followed the woman out of the room. "We haven't been introduced," said Rachel. "My name is Rachel; I'm sorry about your friend."

"I'm Lucretia. Thank you for being sorry, but Nikolai Stepanov is no friend of mine. He works for Boris." They entered her stateroom where Asimov sat on a sofa, wearing headphones. A vodka bottle alongside a half empty glass lay on the table. He smiled when Lucretia entered the room, but frowned on seeing Rachel.

"Rachel will call infirmary to find out how is Nikolai."

"Okay, the phone is there." In his usual abrupt manner, he nodded towards a phone on a desk.

As Rachel picked up the phone, the couple started a conversation in Russian and Asimov embraced Lucretia, speaking softly into her ear.

At least he can be nice, thought Rachel.

Gwen answered the phone and Rachel cautiously explained about the empty tablet bottle she'd found on the floor, checking Asimov wasn't listening. She needn't have worried – he and Lucretia had moved into the bedroom and were having a hushed conversation.

"What are the tablets called?" asked Gwen.

Rachel took the bottle out of her bag and was dismayed at being unable to make out the name due to the writing being in Russian.

Oh well, nothing else for it.

"Mr Asimov, would you mind telling me the name of these tablets, please? The label's in Russian."

Lucretia came into the room, followed by Asimov. "Where did you find this?" she asked.

"I found it on the floor in Nikolai's room. I wanted to tell the doctors in case he's overdosed by accident."

Lucretia took the bottle and her face blushed scarlet. "I'm not sure what you call them in English."

She handed the bottle to Asimov. With a big grin on his face, he looked at Rachel.

"I believe you call them *Viagra* in your country. They are for—"

"Thank you, I realise what they are for."
Rachel spoke into the phone.
"Apparently, they are *Viagra*."

Gwen chuckled at the other end. "I heard! I'll ask Dr Bentley to check – not your usual overdose tablets, but they can cause heart symptoms in large doses."

Rachel put the phone down and looked at Lucretia, avoiding any eye contact with Asimov, who was still chuntering in Russian, finding his own jokes very amusing.

"Thank you for allowing me to use the phone. Nikolai is unconscious, but stable. They're not sure what's wrong with him. If he doesn't improve, they will consider medical evacuation."

"Good riddance," muttered Asimov, drawing a glare from Lucretia.

"I'm sorry for Vladimir's ignorance. Nikolai is not well liked, but we hope he improves and we are relieved that the worst has not happened."

Rachel admired the way Lucretia held herself and wondered what on earth she saw in Vladimir Asimov – except, of course, his being a billionaire.

Each to their own, she thought as she left the stateroom, grimacing to herself at the idea of what an overdose of *Viagra* might do to a person.

Chapter 19

"CODE BLUE, 1512. Repeat, CODE
BLUE, 1512."

Sarah was just changing into formal
uniform after finishing a hectic surgery
when the radio bellowed out the alert.
Bernard was on call, but must need help.
With a deep sigh and adrenaline pumping,
she quickly changed back into her
passenger deck uniform and raced
upstairs to deck fifteen.

I hope it's not one of the Russians, but she
knew intuitively that it would be.

By the time she arrived, Alex and Bernard
were already there. A woman stood
crying hysterically in the corner, and
Sarah saw what looked like a body on the
bed.

"I found him lying there," the woman
screamed. "He's dead."

Alex quickly examined the body while Bernard prepared the defibrillator and resuscitation equipment. Bernard had already cut away the man's shirt for easy access to his chest. A couple rushed in, and the woman tried to console the weeping woman.

"Please, can you take the ladies elsewhere and make sure no-one else comes in?" Sarah instructed the man, who ushered the women out into the corridor.

"There's a pulse," said Alex, relieved. "It's weak, but there is a pulse. He's not breathing, though. Give him some breaths."

Bernard tipped the man's head back and attached a mask to his face, connected to an Ambu bag. He squeezed the bag to give some artificial breaths. Sarah attached oxygen tubing to the bottom of the bag and turned the portable cylinder on to give a high concentration of oxygen.

"If he doesn't breathe, we'll need to intubate," said Alex, sounding stressed. "Where's Dr Bentley?"

They all relaxed as the experienced Dr Bentley arrived and took charge. "What happened?"

"We got an emergency call," said Bernard. "Just as I was finishing a write up, Alex got the call. We dashed up here together."

Alex took over the explanation. "A lady called saying she'd found a man dead. He appeared to be dead, but he has a weak pulse."

"Any signs of an overdose?" Graham asked.

"Not as far as we can see. According to the woman, he was getting ready to escort her to the captain's dinner this evening."

"Any injuries?"

"None. It looks like a heart attack – two young men on one cruise?" Alex sounded exhausted.

"Keep your voice down," hissed Graham.

"He's breathing now," interjected Bernard, "shallowly, but he's breathing on his own.

Sarah had a horrible feeling in the pit of her stomach and walked around the bed, but she couldn't see if there was an injection mark as Bernard had attached a blood pressure cuff to the upper arm.

"Okay, let's deal with what we have." Graham spoke calmly. "Sarah, get a drip in the arm, then we'll get him stretchered down to the infirmary and find out what's happened. For now we'll work on the premise he's had a cardiac event."

Sarah had difficulty putting the needle in the man's arm as the peripheral circulation rapidly shut down, but managed on the second attempt to find a vein. Bernard attached the drip to the cannula once it was in place while Alex and Graham got the stretcher ready.

"Call Gwen, ask her to have a bed ready and a CPAP machine available."

"What is CPAP?" A voice came from the doorway and Sarah noticed the man who had been there earlier.

"Ah, Mr Asimov," acknowledged Graham. "It's a machine that will assist with giving deeper breaths without the need for a ventilator – his breathing is shallow, but he's alive."

"Who is he?" asked Sarah.

"His name is Nikolai Stepanov," answered Bernard. "He is the personal assistant to Mr Boris Stanislav."

At that moment, Boris arrived looking almost as distressed as the woman. Frenzied activity came from the corridor as more and more Russians heard what was happening.

"I think it's time to go," instructed Graham as the crowd grew outside the room. "I'll call you later, Mr Asimov."

Bernard and Alex wheeled the stretcher while Sarah held on to the drip. Graham cleared the corridor ahead, reassuring passengers on the way that everything was under control. As they arrived at the lifts, Rachel came out of one with an anxious man looking like he might faint. Sarah assumed this to be Thomas. Rachel led the man away, giving her a knowing look and mouthing that she would call down to the medical centre later.

Once in the lift heading down to deck two, Graham became very serious, but gave Sarah a warning stare which she took to mean not to mention foul play. By the time they arrived at the infirmary, Gwen was prepared. They transferred Mr Stepanov on to a bed and attached the drip to a stand. His breathing remained shallow, but the bag of fluid had raised his blood pressure, bringing a little colour back to his face.

"What shall I put up next?" asked Sarah.

"Dextrose/saline," replied Graham. "Get a clot buster ready as well, just in case."

Gwen started up the CPAP which would cut in, giving Nikolai Stepanov deeper breaths if his own weren't enough. "Thank goodness for that," said Bernard. "My hand has cramped from squeezing the bag."

"Wuss!" Sarah laughed as the tension lifted because the situation had become less critical.

"Connect the heart monitor," instructed Graham, but Gwen was already on the case. "I'm going to need some blood. Let's do cardiac enzymes, but I want a complete blood screen. We need to know what's going on here."

"We're too far away for an evac aren't we?" asked Alex.

"Maybe, but he's stable now anyway, so let's give it until morning, if anything changes we'll need to consider speeding up or diverting." Medical evacuation was not an option from where they were in the Atlantic and wouldn't be ordered unless necessary and Graham was right: Nikolai Stepanov appeared stable.

"Telephone call for Sister." Raggie appeared in the doorway. Gwen left the room.

Bernard's radio sparked into life again, calling him to a crew member who had trodden on broken glass. "Drunk, I bet," he said. "Is it okay for me to go?"

Graham nodded assent and asked Alex to check the blood results. As soon as they were alone, Graham sprang into action.

"Right, Sarah. You know what we're looking for."

Sarah examined the upper right arm while Graham removed the blood pressure cuff from the left. He let out a deep breath.

"Thank God, nothing." He put the cuff back over Nikolai's arm and relaxed. "For a brief moment, I was terrified we might have a serial killer on board."

Sarah nodded, acknowledging she had been thinking exactly the same. Gwen came back, chuckling to herself.

"Well, I'm glad you've got something to laugh about," snapped Graham.

"I'm sorry. Rachel's just phoned – she found an empty tablet bottle in the man's room and she had to ask Mr Asimov the name of the tablets as the label was written in Russian." She giggled again.

"And?" Graham said impatiently.

"*Viagra.*" She laughed out loud, almost losing control. "The label read *Viagra.*"

Sarah thought Graham was about to lose it, but then he smirked.

"I see. My, my – do we know how many party pills he took?"

"No, but the bottle was empty. Rachel's going to make discreet enquiries and ask his female escort for this evening. He doesn't have a girlfriend – some of the ladies in the group are, erm, paid escorts. Rachel's not sure if that includes sex at present."

"The plot thickens! Next we'll have a brothel on board. The symptoms could be those of a *Viagra* overdose, but I don't think so. We'll bear it in mind. He could also have had illegal tablets concealed in the bottle, which seems more likely, his ECG is normal so are the cardiac enzymes. Is Rachel going to bring the bottle down?"

"Yes, later," replied Gwen.

"Where's Lauren?" asked Sarah.

"Where indeed?" growled Gwen. "She would have got the call at the same time as everyone else. I've just asked for her to be paged again."

Sarah detected Gwen struggling to contain her anger. All medical staff had a duty to respond to a *code blue*, without exception.

The door to the infirmary opened and Lauren breezed in wearing her formal evening uniform.

"There you are," grumbled Gwen, her tone sharp. "Where have you been?"

Graham excused himself while Sarah checked on Nikolai.

"To the captain's party – it was great—" She stopped and looked over at the bed, her face paling. "What happened?"

"What happened is that I called you to an emergency along with every other member of the medical team. As you can see, they are all here, while YOU have only just arrived."

"Who's that in the bed?" Lauren appeared oblivious to Gwen's frustration.

"For your information – his name is Nikolai Stepanov, and had you turned up earlier, you would be fully aware of that and what has happened."

Sarah had never seen Gwen angry and busied herself with Nikolai's charts, pretending not to listen.

"Why did you not respond to your radio?" Gwen appeared to be softening slightly as Lauren looked like she might be ill.

"I muted it."

Whoops, wrong answer! Sarah cringed. She almost felt sorry for the idiotic woman, who hadn't appeared stupid before that moment. Gwen's face reddened and her lips pursed tightly together as she shook her head in disbelief.

"You muted it?" she repeated through gritted teeth. "Perhaps we should continue this conversation in my office." Gwen turned on her heels. Lauren looked over at the man in the bed again, avoiding any eye contact with Sarah, before following Gwen.

"Is it safe?" Graham appeared from the lab area of the ward.

"Coward! Yes, they've gone into Gwen's office," Sarah replied. "I don't expect Lauren will miss a *code blue* again."

"Nor should she," Graham said. "I realise she's new and all, Gwen and I will make allowances for that, but between you and me, one more strike like this and she's out. She's already stepped outside of protocol once – now this."

Sarah wanted to ask what else Lauren had done, but Graham would not be likely to tell her, so she just nodded. Ship policies and procedures were paramount and had to be obeyed without exception. All staff had this drilled into them at induction, and many crew members learned the hard way with misdemeanours resulting in them being escorted off the ship at various ports around the world with no means of getting home. They all knew the rules.

Sarah felt exhausted. She'd only been back for two days, and there had been one suspicious death, one crew member missing, and now the near death of a passenger who was part of an important tour party. Graham looked worn out too – it must be hard for him. He carried the responsibility for the health and wellbeing of all passengers and crew, answerable only to the captain.

Gwen and Lauren came back to the ward.

"You can go now, Sarah," said Gwen. "Lauren will take the night shift and care for Mr Stepanov. Is the patient stable?" Gwen checked with Graham.

"Yes, his cardiac enzymes are normal, as is his heart rhythm, and he's breathing better – I have just stopped the CPAP. He's out of the woods. There doesn't seem to be anything remarkable with the blood results we have so far, either. It's a mystery. Alex will need to repeat the enzymes in a couple of hours."

"Okay, well I'll call it a night, too. Bernard is on call with Alex. Where is Alex?"

"He's gone to visit the passenger with chronic airways disease who might have a chest infection," replied Graham, turning to Lauren. "Any problems, call me, and as soon as he wakes up, I want to speak with him. I don't care what time that is – call me."

"Yes, sir," muttered Lauren, and this time Graham didn't correct her for calling him sir.

Sarah left Lauren after handing over and reminding her where everything in the treatment room was kept. "Give me a shout if you're unsure, I won't mind," she said, trying to be kind.

Lauren rolled her eyes. "I'm a very experienced nurse. I was qualified when you were still at school."

"Of course you are." Sarah walked away. *One who doesn't respond to emergency calls and tries to seduce my friend.* The sympathy train had well and truly left the station as far as Sarah was concerned.

On her way out, she caught sight of Rachel.

"I almost forgot you were coming. Let's go – my room, if you don't mind. I'm beat."

Chapter 20

Rachel went back to Nikolai's room after calling the medical centre and found Thomas and Natalia Fenenko, the woman who had found him. Natalia told them she worked as a paid escort. Boris joined them, jittery and agitated, pacing the room.

"How could this happen?" he repeated over and over.

"Did he have any illnesses?" Rachel asked.

"Not that I knew, he hasn't worked for me too long."

"Is he likely to have taken an overdose?"

"I don't think so – but who knows what goes on inside another man's head?"

"He would not have taken an overdose," said Natalia, emphatically. "I saw him fifteen minutes before to confirm time to meet for dinner. He looked – how you say? – smug. He hummed well-known Russian song; he was happy."

"Perhaps he had a hidden illness," said Boris. "Anyway, I need to find papers Nikolai had, so please excuse me, ladies. See you later, Thomas." He took what appeared to be Nikolai's briefcase and left.

Thomas's colour had returned, but he still seemed incapable of doing anything, so Rachel took over.

"Can I get you a cup of tea?" she asked Natalia.

"I heard you British believe tea is answer to everything, but I would like vodka, please – there is some on his table there." She pointed towards the coffee table.

"Scotch," muttered Thomas, sitting himself down on Nikolai's sofa bed.

After pouring their drinks and opting for bottled mineral water, Rachel sat down next to Thomas and focussed on Natalia. "Thomas will need to write a report for his company. Do you mind telling us exactly what happened this evening? My name is Rachel, by the way."

Natalia explained how Boris had asked her earlier in the day to escort Nikolai to the captain's dinner. "I shouldn't say this, but Nikolai is not nice man, nobody likes him. He keeps requesting me, though, and the pay is good, so I do my job and give him good time."

Rachel assumed that the good time involved staying overnight. "Go on," she encouraged.

"I came to room at six-thirty prompt and knocked. He didn't answer, so I knocked again, loud. When he didn't come, I asked room steward from other room to unlock for me. She swiped door open, then I saw him lying on bed and told him to hurry.

He wasn't moving. He looked white like sheet; I was sure he was dead. I screamed and pressed emergency button on telephone."

"Can you remember anything else? Did you notice this tablet bottle on the floor?" Rachel held up the empty bottle.

"No, I saw nothing except body on bed. I panicked and ran to door after calling for help, waiting for doctor. Male nurse and doctor arrived, then more people. Lucretia and Mr Asimov came to help me and other nurse who arrived asked him to clear room."

"Have you seen the tablet bottle before?" Rachel persisted.

Natalia looked embarrassed. "Yes, last night. He took pill out of drawer before going to bathroom to change."

"Did you see how many pills were in the bottle?"

"Yes, full bottle. I opened drawer to find out what he had taken. I suspected it might be drugs, but realised he needed pills to be man."

Ignoring the scorn, Rachel continued. "Can you think of anything else that appeared strange tonight? Did he seem unwell?"

"He looked well. He was gloating like he had won on horse or something – that is all."

Asimov turned up and suggested they leave Nikolai's room. He advised Natalia to join some of the others in the main restaurant for dinner.

"Thomas, we need to go for the captain's dinner."

Thomas followed him out of the room.

Rachel decided there was nothing more to discover and returned to her room, surreptitiously. She didn't want Asimov to know how close her room was to his.

The evening's events and wondering what had happened to Nikolai were giving her brain ache. What about the empty tablet bottle? An overdose seemed unlikely, considering Nikolai's mood, if Natalia was telling the truth. Unless the bottle contained illegal drugs, and he'd taken an accidental overdose of those.

Perhaps he had a heart attack – it happens.

Rachel headed down to the medical centre and bumped into Dr Bentley on his way out.

"Good evening, Rachel."

"Good evening, Doctor. How is he?"

"Recovering and stable. Sarah's in the infirmary if you're looking for her."

"Thank you. This is the empty pill bottle I found under Nikolai's bed. Natalia, the woman who found him, said it was full last night."

Dr Bentley took the bottle. "Curious! Thank you, Rachel. I don't think it's an overdose, and certainly not with these – the symptoms are all wrong, but I will ask Mr Stepanov about the empty bottle when he wakes." He slipped the bottle into his trouser pocket. Rachel noticed how fatigued he looked.

It can't be easy.

She proceeded through to the waiting room just as Sarah was leaving. They stopped by the buffet on the way to Sarah's room as neither of them had eaten anything substantial since lunchtime.

"I managed a few canapés before everything kicked off," remarked Rachel as she filled a plate with pizza and salad.

"You're lucky, I didn't even manage that. Surgery ran late, and I went to change into formals, but then had to change back when I got the emergency call. Seriously, what a day – again. First Bernard and Lauren, and then this. And Jefgeny is still AWOL – I guess he jumped after all." Sarah didn't pause for breath while filling a plate, choosing a high-fat, high-carbohydrate combo.

"What about Bernard and Lauren?" asked Rachel.

"It's a long story. Last night, Bernard got to his room and passed out, only to find Lauren in his bed this morning. He called me first-thing, beside himself."

"I can't believe it! He seems so happily married."

"Me neither, and what's more, I've never seen him drunk, let alone pass out. But as it turns out, once he explained to Lauren that there would be no repeat – of an event he couldn't remember, by the way – the wretched woman told him nothing had happened anyway because he'd flaked out. He's been floating on air since hearing that news. I still don't understand how he let himself get that drunk, though."

"Maybe he hadn't eaten enough," replied Rachel. "These cruises are becoming a bit too *Agatha Christie* for my liking."

"I know what you mean, but I'm hoping the only murder taking place will be that of Erik Marinov. Although that's one too many, it wouldn't be the first time a falling out among crew has ended up in a death. Rare, but not unheard of."

Rachel chewed over the events of the past two days, unable to take it all in. When they got to Sarah's room, they flopped into chairs and ate. Rachel hadn't realised just how hungry she was until that moment. Her friend looked shattered.

Sarah confirmed Nikolai had stabilised and what had happened with the rather eccentric Lauren.

"Serves her right she's been given the night shift."

"Ooh, that's not like you. She's really got under your skin, hasn't she?"

"I'm sorry, Rachel, but first, she would have taken advantage of Bernard when he's a married man, and then she swans into the medical centre after ignoring a *code blue* and enjoying an evening with the officers without a care in the world. Finally, when I did feel sorry for her and offered support following her rocketing from Gwen, what does she do? Bites my head off and tells me what an experienced nurse she is! I've a good mind to call the hospital where she trained and ask if she bought her qualification. I bet the Africans were glad to get rid of the weirdo."

Rachel laughed out loud following this rant. "I have to give it to her – I've never known anyone wind you up like this. Look, you're exhausted. You've only been back two days and have hardly slept. Get some sleep – we can catch up tomorrow."

"Actually, if you wouldn't mind, that would be great. I can't keep my eyes open much longer. Is there anything you need to tell me?"

"No, nothing that can't wait another day. It looks like the events of tonight are unrelated to your missing crewman." Rachel looked at her watch and realised it was after midnight. "I'll stop by the casino and catch a word with Jefgeny's girlfriend."

Sarah yawned. "Good idea."

Rachel got up to leave and Sarah dragged herself up and walked her to the door where they hugged.

"Catch you tomorrow, then," said Rachel.

After her meal, Rachel had got a second wind and made her way to the casino. She ordered a martini and lemonade, and asked the barman, "Can you tell me if Eva Sipka is working this evening?"

"Yes, she is on the roulette table."

Someone else ordered a drink, giving Rachel the opportunity to take a seat on a barstool with a good view of the roulette table. She took her phone out of her handbag and pretended to look at it. *Carlos would be proud of me,* but she knew he would more than likely be worried she was putting herself in danger. These thoughts did nothing for her concentration.

Arguing with herself that the facts pointed to a murder/suicide eased her conscience. It was time to focus on the woman at the roulette table.

Eva was tall, mid-twenties with long, shiny blonde hair. Although her face was pretty, her flint-like eyes showed a rugged determination. Rachel thought she looked prettier in real life than in the photo Waverley had shown her.

Rachel snapped a few photos with her mobile phone and studied them in close up. This did not appear to be a woman grieving for the father of her child – if she was pregnant. In fact, Eva Sipka radiated happiness, joking with passengers gambling at her table, and with her colleagues. It could have been an act, but Rachel didn't detect any sign of loss.

That woman knows where Jefgeny is.

Chapter 21

"Did you do this?"

Boris looked visibly shaken as he followed Vladimir into his room after the captain's dinner, which had gone well considering the events prior to it. Now Vladimir had to deal with this irritating man instead of dancing with his beautiful Lucretia.

"Lulu, my darling, would you mind giving me a few minutes?" He scowled at Boris, took him by the arm and frog marched him to his own room. "Please keep your voice down, you idiot. Lucretia knows nothing of our deal." He spat the words out while Boris fiddled with his swipe card.

"I will have nothing to do with murder."

"I have no idea what you're talking about," said Vladimir. "Why would I want to murder your PA? Anyway, he's not dead, is he?"

"Don't make out you don't understand why I'm asking. I told you he was blackmailing me. You were aware he wanted twenty thousand euros in return for silence."

"And I told you I would deal with him later," Vladimir barked.

"Exactly, but I didn't realise that meant attempted murder."

"I don't go around murdering people! I meant I would pay him and ensure he gets posted somewhere out of harm's way on our return to Russia. Siberia, perhaps." Vladimir chuckled.

"And that's it? I'm meant to accept you had nothing to do with this?"

Vladimir didn't like being challenged. Trying not to lose control and wishing he had not agreed to help his friend transport documents from the US, he glared at Boris. He had always known there would be risks with an unreliable pawn. Boris was likely to panic and give the game away at any moment, and his sudden belligerence annoyed Vladimir.

"You can believe what you like, but as far as I am aware, Nikolai is ill – unless, of course, *you* had anything to do with it. After all, it's you he is blackmailing."

"Don't be ridiculous!" Boris reddened again. Sweating, he loosened his tie and slumped down in a chair.

At least the idiot had quietened down. "Did you tell anyone else?"

"No, only you. Did you?"

"No, the only people who know about it are you, me and Sergei, who is trustworthy."

"What about your minders? They heard the conversation."

"My minders are well paid – they have no reason to tell anyone else. Look, this is an unfortunate illness. The doctor told me over dinner it was most likely drugs or a heart attack. It is convenient, yes?"

"It would have been more convenient if he'd died," blustered Boris, "but I still want nothing to do with that kind of thing. Just my luck he survived."

Boris put his head in his hands. He looked upset but appeared satisfied with Vladimir's answer.

"Everything will be alright."

"I guess so. I'm worried about breaking the law, that's all – this is a one-off job. You do get that, don't you?"

"Yes, yes," replied Vladimir. *At least, until the next time.*

He smiled to himself as he left the room.

Day 3

Chapter 22

The ship's soporific rocking motion soothed Sarah to sleep as soon as her head hit the pillow. She was in a deep slumber, dreaming of surfing off the coast of Hawaii. The waves enveloped her multi coloured surfboard, along with that of a handsome black-haired hunk. The rise and fall of their surfboards made her feel alive. They were laughing as they approached a monster wave. As they were climbing it, finally nearing the top, her companion became separated from his board and disappeared under the water. He cried out, *"CODE BLUE, INFIRMARY!"*

She woke up sweating in a panic before realising it was a dream.

"I REPEAT, CODE BLUE –
INFIRMARY." The radio bellowing on
her bedside table was not a dream.

Oh no!

She quickly climbed into her scrubs,
taking a gulp of water before diving out of
the room towards the infirmary. She
rushed through the doors to see Bernard
performing CPR while Alex stood at the
head of the bed. Having intubated Nikolai
Stepanov, he was delivering respirations
in between Bernard's cardiac massage.
Graham injected adrenaline directly into
the patient's heart and other drugs through
the IV tube. Gwen was drawing up and
passing drugs as Graham barked out
instructions.

This scene had played out a thousand
times before in hospital casualty
departments, but it was a first for Sarah
on the *Coral Queen*. She took in the
situation in a matter of seconds before

leaping into action, adrenaline and muscle memory taking over.

Sarah ran towards the bed and took over from Bernard, who looked whacked. Cardiac massage was draining, and he looked like he'd been doing it for a while. Lauren was at the foot of the bed, writing down the drugs used on a chart.

"How long?" she asked Bernard.

"CLEAR!" Graham shouted. They all stepped back from the bed and Graham released a defibrillator shock. Nikolai's body jerked as the voltage shot through him, but it made no difference to the heart monitor that continued in a straight line.

"Forty-five minutes. Lauren put out the call; me and Alex were first on scene. Graham and Gwen have been here a while too. He's only had one shockable rhythm, and that was it, but—" Bernard spoke quietly as if Nikolai might hear, "he's not coming round."

Graham had obviously come to the same conclusion as he shook his head and stood back from the bed. "Stop what you're doing, folks." He looked at his watch. "Time of death 04.17. We'll need more blood, fluid and swabs for post mortem and toxicology, Alex. They'll be tested when we hit New York."

Alex nodded and began the process of extracting blood from Nikolai's collapsed veins, along with fluid from the eyes. Lauren recorded time of death on the chart while Gwen removed the leads and tubes from the dead man. This was the first time someone had died in the infirmary and the team looked low, the atmosphere was gloomy. Quiet descended as each person processed the death and performed their various jobs like automatons.

"I'm going to order some coffee from the kitchen," said Gwen. After finishing their tasks and covering the body, they all followed after her, except for Bernard and Sarah.

"We'll move him," said Bernard.

Sarah and Bernard cleaned up the corpse of Nikolai Stepanov and wheeled him through to the morgue.

"I don't like this room," said Sarah. She looked at the six metal doors, each drawer comfortably capable of housing a body until they reached port. In spite of knowing that large cruise ships were required to have a morgue on board, she wasn't happy at the amount of use this one was getting.

"I would think it strange if you did," said Bernard, trying to cheer her up. As soon as they had put the body away in a refrigerated container, he winked at her. "I hope that's the last one – we only have four drawers left."

Sarah thumped his arm playfully, which made them both laugh. They made their way to the office to join the others for coffee.

"I'm really sorry, Gwen, I must have been in a deep sleep."

"Don't worry. We knew you'd been up all night on Saturday – I asked them not to call you at first, but I thought you'd want to know, so I put the call out."

Sarah smiled in appreciation, but noticed Lauren giving her a stony stare. "Thank you," she said to Gwen. Glaring back at Lauren, she added, "That was very thoughtful."

Now you're being childish, she rebuked herself.

"Okay, perhaps now the crisis is over, Lauren can tell us what happened," said Graham as he took a swig of coffee.

All eyes turned towards Lauren. "Everything was quiet, his obs were stable until he woke up and started thrashing about. I tried to calm him down and tell him what had happened, but then he fell back on the bed. I only just managed to stop him falling out. He'd pulled off the monitor leads, so I didn't see his vitals. I tried to rouse him, checked his pulse and airway. There was nothing, so I dialled the emergency through and started to resuscitate. Bernard arrived first, we tried to bring him round. Alex came next, then the rest of you, except for Sarah, who was asleep."

Sarah rolled her eyes at Bernard, who smirked.

"So we don't have a recording of his rhythm before he arrested?" asked Graham.

"No – sorry, sir, I didn't have time to put the leads back until Bernard arrived." Suddenly she started to cry. "We're all going to die! It's Novichok – I've been reading about it on the news. I'm certain this is it, and he coughed all over me before he died."

Graham gawped at her, astonished. "Of course it's not Novichok. The symptoms of a nerve agent death are completely different to what happened here. My dear girl, Russians don't carry nerve agents around like smarties."

"I think perhaps you should go to bed, Lauren," said Gwen, calmly. "You've had a difficult induction into cruise ship life. I can assure you this is far from normal. I concur with Dr Bentley. This. Is. Definitely. Not a nerve agent death, and I must insist that you do not repeat such thoughts to anyone on board ship. We do not want unsubstantiated rumours spreading like wildfire, causing alarm. Are we clear?"

Lauren nodded, wiping her eyes, whimpering.

Alex patted her on the shoulder. "Come on, I'll walk with you. It's most likely a tragic heart attack. You'll feel much better in the morning. It's been a stressful night for all of us."

Lauren heaved herself out of the chair slowly and walked off with Alex.

"Don't take her for a drink," Sarah muttered sarcastically under her breath, but the twinkle in Gwen's eye revealed she'd heard.

"How extraordinary!" Graham was still processing the outburst. "Perhaps working in Africa has warped her vision. I've never heard anything so absurd."

"We'd better keep a closer eye on her," said Gwen to Sarah and Bernard.

"Perhaps she's suffering from stress," said Bernard.

"I suppose it could be PTSD," said Graham. "No signs of it until now, though."

"Maybe she's got an over-active imagination," added Sarah. Unable to understand why she couldn't feel any sympathy towards Lauren, she didn't say any more.

"I'd better go and inform the captain we've had a second death. He's not going to be happy about it. I'll let Mr Stanislav and the tour guide know in the morning. Would you mind hunting out the next of kin, Gwen?"

"Already done, he has a brother in Moscow. I've emailed you the name and number."

"Thank you. Goodnight all. See you in a few hours."

After Graham had gone, Sarah poured another cup of coffee for herself, Gwen and Bernard. "I don't want to sound neurotic, but we are treating this as a natural death, aren't we?"

"I was wondering the same thing," said Gwen. "It's the Rachel influence."

"I refuse to work with a bunch of paranoid nurses." Bernard laughed. "One is quite enough."

"You're right. It was either a heart attack, or an overdose," said Gwen. "There're certainly no nerve agents on board this ship, and our Russian friends are enjoying a nice holiday the same as all the other passengers. Perhaps we're all jittery over the death of Erik Marinov. I don't imagine the two deaths are linked, but I can't help be sad about the tragic deaths of two young men on our watch."

Sarah looked at the time; it was 6am. She excused herself and decided to go and see Rachel for breakfast and fill her in on the night's activities.

Chapter 23

Getting out of the shower, Rachel heard knocking. She grabbed a towel robe and looked through the spyhole. Mario arrived with a pot of coffee just as she opened the door to let Sarah in.

"You're up early! I thought you'd sleep in this morning."

"Yes, I thought I'd keep up with the Princes and join you for breakfast. Is that okay, Mario?"

"Yes, ma'am. I will bring breakfast for two. Would you like cooked as well as cereal and toast?"

"Yes, I would please – I'm famished," replied Sarah.

"Me too, Mario, please," said Rachel.

Mario left and Rachel moved over to the settee and poured coffee for two. Sarah still looked weary.

"He died," Sarah whispered.

"I assume you mean Nikolai Stepanov?" answered Rachel, frowning. "What happened?"

"Suspected heart attack, but it could have been an overdose. Toxicology tests can't take place until we reach New York. Oh Rachel, it's so sad – he was only forty-eight."

"He looked even younger than that, I would have put him in his thirties," said Rachel. "I assume that this one is natural causes?"

"Everything points that way. Lauren says he woke and thrashed about before collapsing so it sounds like it. Afterwards the silly girl became hysterical, suggesting it was Novichok because she'd read about it in the news."

"A slight overreaction then?"

"Not half! As if we don't have enough to deal with without having a paranoid drama queen nobody likes. Rachel, that girl's unhinged."

"If it's any consolation, nobody seemed to like Nikolai either. I certainly didn't, but wouldn't wish him dead."

"Well, let's hope that's all the deaths on this particular sailing. Gwen's blaming you," Sarah said, laughing.

Rachel laughed too. "I was wondering that myself."

"I'm not superstitious, but I do hope there's not a third, although if Jefgeny is dead that would make it three, wouldn't it?"

"Maybe; I'm not sure Jefgeny is dead."

"What makes you say that?"

Mario knocked at the door and came in with a trolley laden with food. "You ladies looked hungry," he explained. "I've brought fresh coffee too."

"Thank you so much, Mario. We'll enjoy this. How is Mr Asimov? I met his girlfriend last night."

"She is nice lady," he replied. "They have early visitors this morning. Dr Bentley is in Mr Asimov's room along with Mr Stanislav and tour guide, Thomas. I am about to take coffee and tea there now. *Bon appétit*, ladies."

"Thank you," said Sarah and Rachel in unison.

Rachel poured milk on her cereal and topped up the coffee cups while Sarah tucked straight into her breakfast. "I never know when I might eat again, and getting up in the early hours always makes me hungry. There's nothing like the smell of fried breakfast and fresh percolated coffee. Anyway, tell me why you don't think Jefgeny is dead."

"I have no proof, but I studied Eva Sipka from a distance last night. The woman just didn't appear to be someone who'd lost the man she loved. Call it a woman's intuition, but I suspect she knows where he is."

"Did you talk to her?"

"No, I only watched. The roulette table was busy with passengers. I suspect the best time to catch her would be at one of the dinner or theatre times, but I will butt out and ask your Officer Waverley to speak with her."

"That's a good idea. The captain wouldn't want you getting involved again and Waverley could get into trouble. Are you still going to spend time with the Russians?"

"A little, but only because I like Thomas. He's fun, and he needs support. He'll take the death of one of his tour party personally."

Rachel and Sarah enjoyed the rest of their breakfast and sat on the balcony for a while, staring out to sea, drinking more coffee. Rachel felt happier when the colour came back to Sarah's face, but was tired herself. The Jefgeny case with its tenuous link to the Russians had been wearing. It was time to put it all behind her. It wasn't her case and there was nothing more to investigate.

Smokescreens weaving in and out of my head, that's all.

"Look at me, still in my bathrobe! I guess I won't be working out today, but I might go for a swim later. Not my favourite, but it could be fun competing for pool space."

"You do that. I'm pleased you're going to keep your head down, Rachel. I'm hoping the medical team gets a quiet spell too – we're bushed. I'll be happy to treat drunks and break up crew brawls rather than come across any more bodies."

"Sounds like a policewoman's lot!" said Rachel.

"Are you okay now? We haven't had a chance to discuss your court case, but can you forget about it?"

"Yes I can, it's over. In fact, Carlos has been nagging me about moving closer to him in London, and my parents would be happy for me to work somewhere in Hertfordshire, so I'll start looking for jobs when I get back. I've given Leeds constabulary four years of my life, so I'm not obligated to stay there any longer." Rachel didn't feel it was the right time to tell Sarah about the threats Tansley had made after the trial; she already had enough on her plate.

"And of course there is always cruise ship security. Waverley would love you on his team. Quite a few of the security team are leaving over the next two years – some are long past retirement age and the cruise line is pressuring Waverley to take on new blood."

"If it weren't for Carlos, I'd jump at the chance right now, but I wouldn't like to be away from him for nine months at a time."

"Sounds serious. I'm so pleased, Rachel. I like Carlos and he's good for you." Sarah didn't say how much she had disliked Rachel's ex-fiancé.

"He is lovely, but I'm still wary of commitment after Robert. I really believed I knew him; it shattered my confidence in my judgement."

"Rachel, you're a great judge of character, but we can all be blind when it comes to love. Trust me, Carlos is nothing like Robert, and from the way he looks at you, I can tell he adores you."

"He is wonderful and Marjorie loves him." Marjorie was a spirited elderly lady Rachel had met on her previous cruise, and they'd remained friends ever since. "Dad's as wary as I am, and he and Carlos prowl around each other like they're on eggshells. Mum says Dad's being overprotective and he'll come round. I do hope so because it's just not helping."

"I'm sure you're right. When the time is right, your dad will embrace Carlos for making you happy after the trauma you went through before. Anyway, I'm not sure where the time's gone, but I'd better sneak back to my room and get out of these scrubs before anyone sees me. Surgery starts in an hour."

"Are you on call?"

"No, Gwen's taking Lauren's on call as she's worried about her state of mind. Graham's on for the docs. Shall we meet for afternoon tea or in the jazz bar tonight?"

"Both, if you're free."

"Great – see you at three."

Sarah left and Rachel dressed, putting her bikini on under her clothes. It was time to pay Waverley a visit before getting back into holiday mode.

He was at his desk typing on his computer when he spotted her.

"Come in," he called. "Miss Prince," he coughed, "sorry, Rachel. Please don't tell me you're the bearer of bad news today."

"No, not exactly. I'm not sure I have any news, just a hunch."

Rachel didn't miss the caution on his face. "Take a seat and tell me about your *hunch*." He moved away from his desk and came round to the comfy chairs. Rachel joined him and told him about her observation of Jefgeny's girlfriend last night and her suspicion that Eva might know where Jefgeny was hiding.

"If he is hiding," she finished.

"I see – and you base all this on the premise that the woman looked happier than you would expect?"

Flushing, Rachel answered. "When you say it like that, it sounds odd, but yes, that's all I've got to offer."

"She has an appointment with Dr Romano this morning to determine whether she is pregnant. The best I can do for you is to ask him what he makes of her emotional state. We have already interviewed Ms Sipka, and she seems genuinely distraught – perhaps she's good at her job and manages to hide her grief. We are certain Jefgeny Popov is no longer on the ship. My team have even searched the lifeboats to make sure he's not hiding in any of these. He killed Erik Marinov after a row, and afterwards, filled with remorse, he threw himself overboard. That's my conclusion." Waverley emphasised his conviction by slamming a folder down on his desk.

Rachel understood his logic, but she still had her doubts about the facts. In spite of this, she determined not to get entangled in something that was not her concern. Waverley had become silent, making it clear her suspicions were something he didn't want to hear.

"Thank you for seeing me." Rachel left his office a fraction irritated by his attitude. "Well, CSO Waverley, I've done my civil duty. Now it's down to you," she mumbled to herself as she made her way towards the lido deck.

Chapter 24

A balmy day greeted Rachel out on deck, the ship rocking gently back and forth as soothing cross-waves passed underneath. Perching on a sun lounger overlooking the busy pools, she spent the morning sunbathing on the lido deck. The sun's rays reflected off two deep blue swimming pools, with crowds rushing in to take advantage of the opportunity to swim or bask in the sunshine. In the captain's morning bulletin, he'd said the temperature would be twenty-six degrees centigrade, providing plenty of heat even with the gentle sea breeze that swept across the deck every so often.

Waiters and pool attendants carried out their daily tasks efficiently and appeared whenever anyone was thirsty. Beefy aromas from the grill bar wafted down, reminding her she was hungry, but Rachel decided to make a move to the salad bar in the main buffet. The fried breakfast had provided more than enough fat for one day.

She pulled a summer dress over her bikini, picked up her book and vacated the sun lounger. On entering the buffet area, she had her hands squirted with hand disinfectant by a waitress – one of the many routines that took place on board a ship.

"Rachel!"

She turned around. Thomas was carrying a tray of what looked like Jamaican food.

"Hello, Thomas."

"Join me over there when you've got your food." He nodded towards a window table for four. Boris sat tucking into his lunch.

"Okay, see you in a minute."

There was a Jamaican theme today, and the staff were wearing brightly coloured clothing to match it. A diverse selection of Jamaican delicacies was on display and she opted for a jerk chicken fillet to accompany her salad before negotiating her way to where Thomas and Boris were sitting.

"Did you hear about Nikolai?" Thomas asked.

Rachel wasn't sure whether she would be betraying Sarah's confidentiality if she replied honestly, so she carried on chewing, showing she couldn't speak.

"I'm afraid Nikolai passed away," Boris whispered.

"I'm so sorry," said Rachel. "That must be terribly upsetting for your party."

"Not really, people didn't like him and they didn't know him well. They are sad that someone has died, but not enough for it to be of any great concern."

Rachel stared in shock at his easy dismissal of the tragedy. Thomas explained.

"Russians aren't afraid to say what they think, Rachel. Unlike us, they are not constrained by politeness. That doesn't mean they're not concerned by the sudden death of one of their group, and Mr Stanislav has found the incident very distressing."

"Yes, it is most inconvenient. He has left me without a personal assistant for the rest of the cruise. It has been big upset for Natalia Fenenko, the poor girl who found him. She is very shaken."

"Have they said what caused his death?" Rachel asked.

"It was a heart attack or an overdose," answered Thomas. "They won't know for certain until he has a post-mortem. The family have requested repatriation to Russia for that, which the cruise line has agreed to. The insurance company will foot the bill and his brother is flying to New York to return home with the body."

"I see," said Rachel. "How is Natalia today?"

"She is okay; the ladies are taking her for pampering session in health spa," said Boris. "Russian ladies enjoy pampering. You are welcome to join them for some time, Miss Prince."

"Thank you, that's kind – I'll bear it in mind." Rachel detected a degree of agitation emanating from Boris and wondered what was on his mind.

They were distracted by sudden 'Oohs' and 'Ahs' as people gravitated towards the windows. Rachel followed their gaze and saw a large pod of dolphins swimming beside the ship.

"Aren't they gorgeous?" she exclaimed.

"Oh, they're awesome." Thomas beamed from ear to ear. Even Boris was smiling.

"Amazing creatures, and so intelligent," he said. "They are catching fish that ship is disturbing."

They remained transfixed by the spectacular display right before their eyes as the dolphins leapt through the air, diving in and out of the water.

The pod eventually disappeared from view.

"Now you wouldn't see that from an airplane," remarked a gleeful Thomas. He looked carefree again, and the sombre moments had passed. Boris still had a faraway look in his eyes as if something was weighing on his mind, but he returned to the present and smiled at Rachel and Thomas.

"If you will excuse me, I have some business to attend to."

"See you for the group massage, 4pm," Thomas called after him. Rachel gave him a look.

"Group massage?"

"Men only." He winked, then more seriously, he remarked, "To be honest, it will help them chill out. There's been too much tension in the air, particularly between Mr Asimov and Boris, and Sergei pops up from nowhere with alarming regularity. I swear that man never smiles – a more dour face, I've never encountered. Honestly, group dynamics, Rachel – be thankful you can hop in and out."

"I can't say I'd want to be around the sour-faced Asimov for very long, and Boris looks to be in a world of his own. Is Sergei the tall man with grey hair and beard?"

"Yes, that's him."

"I've noticed him from time to time. What does he do and where does he fit in?"

"As far as I'm aware, he's a businessman who part-owns some businesses with Mr Asimov. It's funny, I heard some of the others say he was at Yale at the same time as Nikolai, but they never spoke. That said, Sergei is older than him, so perhaps they never met."

"Still, you would expect old Yalies to have something to say to each other," remarked Rachel. "Maybe he imagined Nikolai was below him, being a PA."

"He seems to think everyone is below him. The party is generally more at ease when only one of the big three is present."

"Even happier when none are there, I suspect," said Rachel, laughing.

"Indeed. Anyway, I'm afraid I need to meet some of the ladies in the casino for a Blackjack lesson."

"Oh, can I come too?" The words were out of her mouth before she could stop them. *It can't do any harm, and perhaps Eva is off duty.*

"Please do. I hate gambling, but needs must." He held out his arm for Rachel to take.

On arrival at the casino, they saw a few men from Thomas's party and two women, none of whom Rachel had spoken to before. She recognised Eva Sipka coming towards them.

"Hello, I'm Thomas the tour guide, we're all here now."

"We will have the lesson on the other side of barrier."

Staff had put a makeshift security rope in place to cordon off an area of the casino, preventing other passengers entering. Thomas, Rachel and the rest of the group followed Eva. Rachel still didn't detect any sadness in the woman's demeanour or eyes.

The eyes are the window to the soul, her father had always told her, and she believed it. These eyes sparkled. *She is pregnant, then,* thought Rachel.

"Please, ladies and gentlemen, take seats around the table."

The table formed a large semi-circle in shiny mahogany with a golfing-green cloth cover. The group positioned the padded low-back stools around the semi circular part. Rachel climbed up on to one next to Thomas. There were seven of them in all, and they stretched around the table while Eva moved to stand behind the flat edge.

It took the next thirty minutes to learn the rules of Blackjack and have a few practice games. Rachel found herself interested in the psychology of the game in spite of having a natural aversion to gambling. It was interesting to learn that despite them all playing against the dealer, the actions of one player could have a detrimental impact on other players, who might lose money when someone made the wrong call.

"You will find other players become impatient with you if you keep doing this," Eva explained.

Thomas nudged Rachel. "I might give it a go tonight, just to annoy people."

"You wouldn't!" The evil twinkle in his eye gave him away. It was such a pity he had to be with a serious group – he would be much better with party lovers. She felt sorry for him.

Some of the group lost interest towards the end of the game – in all likelihood, they knew how to play already. They dispersed, leaving Thomas, Rachel and one other man called Marat.

"Where you from?" Marat asked Eva.

"Slovenia, but I was born in Croatia. My parents moved to Slovenia when I was three."

"I have an uncle in Slovenia," Marat continued. "You are not wearing ring. No husband back home?"

Rachel noticed a brief flicker of unease.

"I hope to marry soon." Eva instinctively put her hand over her abdomen as if reassuring her unborn baby.

"Good luck with that. I had two wives – no more." He laughed.

"Until the next time, he means," joked Thomas.

Marat slapped Thomas on the back. "He's right – until the next time."

At this point, Marat got up and left the table, accepting defeat on the chat-up front. Thomas looked ready to leave too, but Rachel wanted to take advantage of the turn in the conversation.

"Does your boyfriend work on the ship?" she asked Eva, who looked around as if to check no-one was listening.

"He did, but no longer." Apprehension crossed the young woman's face.

"Will you return to Slovenia when you marry?"

"I hope to live in America. What about you? Do you have a boyfriend? You are very beautiful."

"How do you know I'm not her man?" asked Thomas.

Rachel suspected Eva had sussed Thomas out.

"My boyfriend is back in England, his name is Carlos," Rachel answered.

"She's breaking my heart," said Thomas, reaching for her hand.

"Eva – time for a break." A young woman with dark-brown hair tied in a ponytail approached the table.

"Thank you for the lesson." Thomas led Rachel away. "Sorry to desert you, but I'd better go for my man massage."

"Enjoy yourself," Rachel answered, but was miles away, mulling over the conversation with Eva, and more convinced than ever Jefgeny was still alive.

Waverley will have to believe me now.

Chapter 25

While she was on her way towards the main atrium, a man bumped into Rachel, causing her to drop her bag and spill its contents.

"I'm so sorry." The man stooped down to help her pick things up. "I can't have been looking where I was going."

"No harm done. Do I know you from somewhere?"

"I don't think so, unless you come from Nottingham?"

"No," she replied. "Anyway, thank you for helping. Goodbye." Tucking the clutch bag under her arm, she went in search of Sarah. She caught sight of her friend seated at a table for two by a window, staring out at the Atlantic.

"Penny for your thoughts," said Rachel as she leaned in to embrace her friend.

Sarah smiled up at her as she took the seat opposite. "Just daydreaming, wondering whether it was wise to take on another nine-month contract."

"But you love the work," Rachel said.

"I do usually, but these past few days have been extremely difficult. I don't feel like I've been off duty at all, I'm grumpy all the time, and on top of that, we now have an unreliable and peculiar colleague to cover for." Sarah lowered her voice to a whisper.

Noticing the strain telling on her friend's face, Rachel tried to encourage her. "Well tonight you're off and we'll enjoy a nice dinner – how would you like to go to the Steakhouse?" Sarah loved steak.

"Oh, I'd love that. Don't mind me, I'm just having a moment. How's your day been?"

"It's been good." Rachel decided not to mention the Jefgeny thing. "I lazed about sunbathing all morning, had lunch with Thomas. He makes me laugh, so I'm behaving like quite the cruise passenger! We even spotted a pod of dolphins that put on a spectacular display for everyone in the buffet."

Sarah cheered up. "That's great, Rachel. Actually my day has been alright, apart from the lack of sleep. I saw children in morning surgery and made them laugh – they love getting good children stickers and cartoon plasters."

A waiter came along and took Rachel's order for tea, and she chose a chocolate cake from his trolley. Sarah opted for a waffle and strong coffee.

"It's amazing how much food is available. Where do they store it all?" asked Rachel.

"It's more difficult for six sea days as there aren't any stops to stock up, but there are huge storage facilities below decks with great big industrial freezers, fridges and racks of food. Every item of food is monitored, though, and they do run out sometimes when a particular meal is popular – then it's frantic for the kitchen staff."

"I don't know how the waiters manage those trays stacked high with dinners either."

"Trust me, they don't always. You'll hear the occasional clatter of metal when an accident occurs. I'm sure you'll witness one at some stage, but they are amazing and well trained by the hospitality officers."

As they finished their drinks and food, Sarah yawned. "I'm going to head back to my room to catch a nap before evening surgery. Shall we meet at eight?"

"That sounds perfect, I'll see you then – enjoy your sleep."

Rachel took a deep breath before heading downstairs to see if Waverley was in his office. He had a passenger with him, but motioned for her to wait outside, so she found a seat overlooking the sea.

Passengers milled along the corridors en route to destinations or activities. She watched a teenager whose parents were arguing about whether she could go off on her own to explore while they attended a quiz in the Sky view lounge. People appeared happy. Rachel felt relaxed sitting there, but couldn't help being inquisitive regarding Jefgeny's whereabouts, and why he might be hiding. Did he kill his friend? Waverley seemed certain he had, but Sarah said they were close and she was worried about Jefgeny's health. Sometimes the most obvious explanation was the true one, but Rachel couldn't help wondering…

Waverley's door opened, and the passenger shook his hand, thanking him for his time. He gestured for her to come in.

"I suppose you want to ask where I've got to regarding Eva Sipka?" he said. Not waiting for a reply, he continued. "Miss Sipka is pregnant, Dr Romano says she's ecstatic. She told him she would like to vacate the ship in New York as she has relatives living in North Carolina. Dr Romano says she's twelve weeks pregnant, and he's advised her to get a scan at sixteen weeks. He asked who the father was, and she admitted it to be Jefgeny Popov. Dr Romano can find no evidence she believes Mr Popov is still alive. In fact, he says she broke down when he mentioned him."

An Oscar winning performance, no doubt!

Rachel paused before shattering Waverley's happy 'case solved," dream. "I met Eva Sipka this afternoon when I joined a few of Thomas's tour party for a Blackjack lesson."

A frown appeared on Waverley's face. "Why do I feel this will ruin my day?" He gave a wry smile.

"Ms Sipka was unaware I knew anything about her situation, and as one of the men asked her a few innocent questions about boyfriends and so on, she opened up. She made it quite clear she expects to marry soon, and that she plans to live in the United States. There was no mention of the pregnancy, but she talks about a boyfriend in the present tense."

Waverley's face reddened, then he coughed. "She could have been spinning a yarn for the passenger's sake – she's hardly going to say her boyfriend is missing."

"You're right, but why say anything at all, and why flower the story with marriage and settling in America? You said yourself she asked to disembark in New York. Is that usual? If she's on her own with the father of her child presumed dead, surely she would want to work for as long as possible and return home to Slovenia to give birth? You also said Jefgeny's passport was missing."

Waverley put his head in his hands. "If what you are saying is true, we have a suspected murderer on board this ship and a crew member harbouring him." His voice raised a pitch.

"I'm afraid so," answered Rachel.

"Then I need to speak to the captain and bring her in for questioning."

"You could do that."

"I take it you don't agree?"

"Only that Eva's not the type of woman to give up the man she loves and the father of her child, and we can't prove she's hiding him. We only have a supposition. She's more likely to drop her guard when it appears no-one is looking for Jefgeny. At some point, Eva will tell a friend or lead you to him, if you're patient."

"I suspect you're right, but I will need to ask the captain's permission to follow her. Unfortunately she knows the security officers. I can't ask you to follow her because you're not allowed in the staff areas – we do have a new woman in training who Ms Sipka won't have met. This officer can keep watch, but if we have not found Popov by Friday, I will have to question her. Please keep out of this now, Miss Prince, and enjoy the rest of your cruise."

"That's fine by me, Officer Waverley."
Two can play formal.

Rachel dressed for dinner in a turquoise cocktail dress, this time using straighteners on her hair to rein in the waves appearing from too much sun. After applying a smattering of makeup, she was ready. The dark lines that had been under her eyes had all but disappeared and the sparkle had reappeared. The Tansley matter had passed from her mind, and a new job was the top priority after the holiday. She had already spent an hour looking at vacancies in the Metropolitan Police force, and also in Hatfield, not too far from London, and close, but not too close to her parents. It would be cheaper to live there than in London, too.

Entering the main atrium, she browsed around Customer Services before sitting for a while, admiring the shiny marble pillars circling the entertainment area where passengers congregated day and night while the ship sailed. She helped herself to an A4 sheet of daily news snippets from the UK. Deck four formed a part of the tiered atrium, also visible from deck five which encircled the area where Rachel now sat. It was accessible via a spiral staircase and a viewing lift that ran up through the centre of the ship for those who wished to admire each of the main passenger entertainment decks.

Rachel saw Sarah walking towards her and stood to greet her. The colour had returned to Sarah's cheeks. Her brown eyes shone against the backdrop of the white uniform and her brown hair was tied loosely back and perched on top of her head.

"You look much better, and beautiful." They hugged.

"You don't look so bad yourself. Come on, let's go eat. I'm ravenous again."

They walked up two flights of stairs to deck six and on to the steakhouse. As Rachel had pre-booked, the waiter led them to a table for two next to a window, away from the main eating area. Sarah had to be discreet in passenger areas and preferred not to draw attention to herself.

"This is perfect," said Sarah, choosing to sit behind a pillar with her back to the other tables.

"I thought you'd like it. I explained to the manager you would be joining me and we wanted a private area. He was very nice."

"That would be Martin Lonsdale, he's popular with passengers and staff."

"He called himself Marty," said Rachel.

"Yep, that's him. He worked in Vegas at some of the top steakhouses there."

"My mouth's watering already." Rachel concentrated on the menu.

A waiter appeared at the table. "Can I get you anything to drink, ladies?"

"Are you happy with Shiraz?" Rachel asked Sarah.

"Yes, that's fine, and a jug of water with ice, please."

The waiter left them to decide on their meals and returned with the water and the wine, asking Rachel to taste.

"Now I get to practise what I learned at the wine tasting session yesterday. Okay, I first have to check the wine's clear from above. Now I tilt the glass and scrutinise it against the white tablecloth." She was having fun with this, and the waiter was encouraging her.

"Next, ma'am, the smell."

"Yes, I smell it – this one smells spicy – and now my favourite part: the taste." Rachel took a small sip and swilled it around her palate before swallowing. "You know, that's not half bad!" she exclaimed.

"Thank goodness you didn't spit it out like they do when tasting more than one!"

Rachel nodded to the waiter, and he poured wine into both of their glasses before setting the bottle down on the table. He also poured them some water.

They ordered steak dinners, both opting for T-bone which included fillet and sirloin. Rachel asked for well-done and Sarah requested medium. The smell of steak filtering through the restaurant made Rachel feel hungry.

"I rarely eat steak, so this is a real treat for me, and I never eat T-bone, it's too expensive."

"Last time on board, I ate in here twice. Once with Daniel, the guy I dated for a while."

"Have you heard from him since he moved ships?"

"I get the occasional email, but he's not the one for me. That man's still out there, somewhere," answered Sarah, smiling.

"It's good to see you smile," said Rachel. "You've had a torrid return to cruise ship nursing."

"Yes, but today's been more normal. The sleep helped. The only irritation is that one of the Russians, Sergei Markov, has lost his insulin again. Lauren's taken him another vial from the ship's supply and Graham has given him a lecture on safeguarding medicines."

"Isn't that dangerous if a child should find it?"

"It's not ideal, but unless the child has a syringe and needle, they would be unlikely to come to any harm. Anyway, he thinks he threw it out in the trash with a tissue he'd used to wipe blood away. Probably drunk too much vodka."

"Yes, Mario says they like their vodka."

Rachel and Sarah enjoyed a succulent steak dinner and Rachel finally told Sarah about the threat Tansley had made after he'd been found guilty. Her friend looked alarmed.

"Is he dangerous?"

"He's small-time, I suspect, but there have been rumours of links to a drugs gang. I'm hoping he'll forget all about me, and anyway – I've made the humungous decision to find a job in the south."

"Oh, that's a relief. Does anyone else know about the threat?"

"No, I got an anonymous letter attached to the windscreen of my car. I can't even prove it came from him. I just know it was."

"You should tell Carlos and your senior officer, just in case."

"You're right. I didn't want anyone to think I was overreacting; I was so pleased the trial was done and dusted, I put it out of my mind. Carlos and my parents seemed worried enough about me coming on another cruise, I didn't want to make things any worse for them. Carlos has been under a lot of strain himself with a case he's working on."

"That's just like you, Rachel, always putting other people first."

"Pot and kettle comes to mind," said Rachel, laughing.

"Well I'm pleased you'll be leaving Leeds if it will be dangerous for you to stay there."

They finished their desserts and both had a Baileys.

"Drink up, Sarah. I've had an idea."

Chapter 26

"You can't be serious, Rachel!" Sarah's voice had taken on a screeching sound. "What if someone sees me? I could lose my job."

"The room's been untouched, waiting for forensics on land after the ransacking. There might be something in there that would give us a clue." Rachel didn't want to get Sarah into trouble, but was desperate to find out what had happened to Jefgeny.

"Rachel Prince, Waverley will not like this one little bit. Neither will Graham, for that matter."

"You want to find out what happened to Jefgeny? He might be lying ill somewhere." Rachel cringed at using emotional blackmail on her best friend. Sarah looked exasperated as she chewed her bottom lip, something she always did when pondering an issue. Rachel had first noticed it when they'd shared a flat together at university.

"Come on, then, let's go."

"Now?"

"You asked for it, and this is the best possible time, while most of the crew are still at work. Evenings and mornings are their busy times. Those not working will be in the crew bar or café. You'll need to change, otherwise you'll stick out like a sore thumb."

Rachel knew better than to argue the toss now, so meekly followed Sarah back to her room where her friend handed her a set of blue scrubs.

"You're kidding?"

Sarah shrugged, eyebrows hitting the ceiling. "Are you coming or not? Besides, you'll look good in scrubs."

Rachel gave her a look. "Don't push it!" She obediently donned the pale-blue trousers and short-sleeved top.

"Welcome to my world – here, put these trainers on. You can't wear those heels." Sarah was clearly enjoying this now. The trainers were a half-size too small for Rachel and pinched her toes, but they would have to do.

"Stay close and keep your head down if we pass anyone. You'd better tie your hair up. Use this."

Rachel tied her hair into a ponytail with the blue hair bobble. "At least it matches," she said, laughing.

"I always accessorise!"

"Yep, forgot that."

Sarah checked the coast was clear. Rachel followed her to the end of the corridor and through a door marked STAFF ONLY. Once through the door, Rachel resisted the temptation to take a peek in the crew bar.

They descended the same steps she had trodden during her engineering tour. At least she assumed they were, otherwise they were identical. When they reached a deck three floors below the waterline, Sarah slowed, motioning for her to stay still while checking the corridor. The noise level had risen, the grinding of metal extinguishing any sound from their rubber soles. Rachel stifled a cough as musty smoke residues irritated the back of her throat. Hoping it wouldn't make her gag, she regretted not having drunk more water during dinner.

About halfway along this narrow corridor, they came to a door screened off with yellow tape marked: SECURITY DO NOT ENTER. Rachel's heart beat faster as the realisation of what they were doing and the trouble they might get into sank in. She pictured her and Sarah being thrown off ship in New York and wondered whether to suggest they turn back, but Sarah had already opened the door. As a ship's nurse, Sarah carried a universal swipe key that would open any room on board in case of emergency.

Sarah held the door open. "Come on, quick," she hissed.

Rachel paused, but boots and voices entering the corridor further down removed any doubts and caused her to dive into the room and close the door. She stood with her back to it.

"Someone's coming."

Sarah's face looked deathly pale as they waited. The footsteps got louder and Rachel could almost hear her own heart thumping above the noise before the footsteps passed by the room and proceeded on their way.

"Must have been crew," said Sarah. "Right, let's get on with this. What are we looking for?"

"No idea, let's take a peek around. Good grief! It's so small in here, and dark. Where's the light?"

Sarah turned the light on, which cast shadows around the room, but didn't make it bright. "This is how it was when Erik was found. His was the lower bunk. Security packed his belongings, which are now in the purser's office." Sarah was staring sadly at the bed.

Rachel surveyed the room, taking in the scene. Cramped with single bunk beds against one wall, it had a small table with bottle stains and an ashtray still containing cigarette butts. Clothes were scattered on the floor from the ransacking on the day Jefgeny went missing.

That might have been Jefgeny throwing things together before going into hiding, thought Rachel.

"You search his pockets while I check the bathroom – you're the policewoman," said Sarah, handing Rachel a pair of surgical gloves while putting on a pair herself.

"Hm, nurses would make good criminals," Rachel teased, before turning out Jefgeny's pockets. Whoever had ransacked the room had emptied most of the contents on to the floor, so she found nothing.

She picked up a newspaper and checked for any writing or clues, but there were none. There wouldn't be any documents as Waverley would have those locked away.

"Found anything?" Sarah asked.

"No, nothing. You were right, there's nothing here." Rachel bent down to pick up a photograph frame from the floor and saw a photo of two men in high spirits, dressed as pirates in a port somewhere. "Is this Jefgeny and Erik?"

Sarah took the frame. "Yes, that's Jefgeny on the left and Erik on the right."

There was another small photo frame on the floor with a photo of Jefgeny and Eva.

"The ship photographers sometimes do snaps for the crew as keepsakes," explained Sarah.

"I don't think we're going to find anything here – unless all the films I've ever watched are true!" Rachel removed the photo of the two men from the frame, checking the back. Nothing. "Or not." She laughed, then she removed the back of the portrait of Jefgeny with Eva and saw something folded in half. "Jackpot!" she exclaimed.

Sarah came and sat beside her on the lower bunk bed. "What is it?"

Rachel opened the faded piece from a newspaper which contained another photo of two young men, standing either side of a pretty young woman with two small children. One of the men had long hair and a beard and moustache. The photo was in colour, although faded.

"The one on the right is Jefgeny. Do you agree?"

Sarah took the photo. "Yes, the red hair is a giveaway, and the woman has red hair too. I wonder who the others are."

Rachel looked at the picture again. "The other man looks familiar, but I can't place him. He's obviously the woman's husband or partner because they're holding hands."

"Perhaps they are Jefgeny's family or friends. The woman could easily be his sister," suggested Sarah.

"But why hide the photo?" Rachel was preoccupied, playing with the old piece of American newspaper in her hand when the headline jumped out at her.

PROMINENT BUSINESSMEN FOUND GUILTY. Two key witnesses go into witness protection after giving evidence in data theft trial.

Rachel skimmed the article, describing a trial involving a conspiracy to steal plans of a driverless car blueprint from Future Motors, a major company in the USA. The article revealed that a man called Marian Krokowsky, an industrial engineer, and a Russian scientist named Jerzy Bobrinsky had entered witness protection. The US granted Krokowsky citizenship, and Bobrinsky defected. The prototype blueprint was worth an estimated one billion dollars, and Krokowsky and Bobrinsky had revealed the names of two prominent US senators, a US industrial espionage gang leader and his son, along with four Russian businessmen and politicians. The police had intercepted the handover, thanks to information provided by Krokowsky and Bobrinsky, resulting in four of the men being jailed for thirty years each. Two of the Russians working at the Russian embassy had had diplomatic immunity and were deported back to Russia. The rest were given jail terms of various lengths.

Sarah read the article over Rachel's shoulder. "Blimey! This is bigger than we imagined."

"Yes, I suspect that Krokowsky or Bobrinsky took on the new name of Jefgeny Popov, which is why you and Waverley had so little information about his past. Krokowsky, probably, as he was the industrial engineer. The man and woman in the picture must be related to Jefgeny, and it may be all he has left of his past. If Jefgeny is in witness protection, he would have had to sever all links with family. What a comedown, though, from industrial engineer to this."

Rachel looked around the room.

"Perhaps it's where he felt safe, and at least he was still using his engineering skills, getting three square meals plus full board and lodgings with a salary on top. If you think about it, a cruise ship is a great place to remain anonymous."

"Someone found out, though, and killed his friend."

"Do you suppose they were trying to frame him?"

"Or maybe Erik was killed by mistake."

"We have to tell Waverley, but I'm likely to lose my job for breaking ship's rules."

"I agree, we do need to tell Waverley. Can I sleep on it, Sarah? I want to think it through some more, and I'll work out a way of getting Waverley to show me this room without involving you. I want to try to keep you out of it." Rachel placed the photo back inside the paper and folded it up, after taking photos of all the evidence on her mobile phone. She placed the frames back on the floor where she had found them.

Sarah checked the corridor again, and they made their way swiftly back upstairs to her room. Rachel changed her clothes and hugged her friend.

"I'll work something out. It could still be a murder/suicide with no connection to Jefgeny's past." She sounded more reassuring than she felt.

"Thanks, Rachel, but if not, I'll just have to face the consequences. Waverley needs this information in case there is a connection." Sarah's eyes filled up and Rachel was ashamed at having dragged her into this.

"Yes, he does, but there will be a way of telling him without involving you, I'm sure."

Rachel left her friend, determined to protect her somehow.

What the heck is going on? Where are you, Jefgeny Popov?

Day 4

Chapter 27

At one stage during the night, Rachel could hear shouting in the corridor, but it settled down quickly. Restless at the startling discovery in Jefgeny's room, she pressed the button on her phone to check the time and groaned: 3am.

Turning over to get a drink of water, she heard someone trying the door of her room. Rachel leapt out of bed and raced to the door, peeping through the spyhole. The dark-brown hair of a man's head was just visible as he swiped the door and pressed the handle, but Rachel always double locked so no-one could get in. She frantically tried to control her breathing while watching the handle move again.

The man swiped repeatedly while she slowly took off the double lock and pulled the door open. Seeing the look of surprise on his face, she squared up to him.

"Who are you?" she demanded. He looked familiar, but appeared to be drunk.

"Sorry, I must have the wrong room," he slurred and staggered.

"Yes, you have," said Rachel, turning to shut him out. Before she had a chance to move away, the man put his foot in the door. Grabbing her, he spun her backwards, holding a knife to her throat. It all happened so quickly, she had no time to react.

He pinned her tight, walking her back through the room, holding the knife to the front of her neck.

"PC Prince, you have a debt to pay," he snarled in her ear.

Rachel's brain was doing somersaults, trying to work out why he looked familiar. Sucking in air, she croaked, "What are you talking about?" Her mouth was parched, but she figured the longer she kept him talking, the more chance she might have of disarming him. The blade was sharp against her neck, restricting her movement.

"My brother sends his regards."

"Tansley!"

"That's right. He would have come himself, but he's otherwise engaged. But you know all about that, don't you?"

The man walked her towards the balcony.

Not again! What is it with people trying to throw me overboard? She had found herself in the same predicament on her previous cruise. Seeing the irony of the situation, she burst into uncontrollable laughter.

Taken aback by her hysteria, the man loosened his grip. "Oh, you think it's funny, do you? Perhaps you'll be less amused when you take an early morning dip."

Rachel seized the opportunity as the man relaxed his grip to open the curtains. She quickly moved her left hand up against her chest, grabbing his right hand, and rotated his arm, keeping it close to her chest. She then bent forward and slipped behind him in rotation, still holding his right arm close to her, so that the knife was pointing upwards, away from her. As she twisted his arm, he dropped the knife, and she was able to deliver a swift blow to the back of his neck with both of her hands. He lost his balance for a moment and she kicked the knife away before picking up a chair and hitting him hard.

He still lunged at her, just like his brother had done. Managing to avoid the blow from his fist hitting her full in the face, she grabbed his hand and twisted his arm hard behind his back. Using all her strength, she carried on twisting until he cried out in pain.

"Better men than you have tried this before." She spoke through gritted teeth. Without releasing her grip, she pushed him towards the door. "Now open it."

He pulled the door open. Her lungs bursting from the effort of holding his arm in the same position, she pushed him along the back corridor to Asimov's room.

"Let go, pig!" he cursed.

"Knock on the door," she ordered. He knocked with his left hand, and Rachel was relieved when Tweedledum came out of another room. Tweedledee answered Asimov's door at the same time. An astonished silence ensued for a split second until Rachel broke it.

"Can one of you hold him while I call security?"

They grinned. "With pleasure." Tweedledee picked Tansley up and thrust him against a wall. "Would you like to fight me?" He pushed his face up against the man's nose. Tansley looked terrified now.

"No."

"Shame, I like to fight cowards who hit women." He punched the man hard in the stomach to show he meant business. Rachel grimaced as Tansley fell to the floor.

Asimov arrived at the door in his dressing gown and stared at Rachel, who had scratches to her arms and neck and a bruise to her face. Suddenly feeling exposed wearing her scanty nightclothes, but thankful for the two-piece shorts and shirt, Rachel started trembling.

Lucretia appeared. "What are you men doing? Bring her in here." She covered Rachel with a bathrobe. "Call security, Vlad."

Asimov did as he was told while the twins guarded the attacker who remained on the floor of the corridor. Two security guards arrived, and after taking a brief history from Rachel, took Tansley away. They told Rachel the CSO would come up to visit her within the hour.

Asimov looked confused, but Lucretia remained practical. She sat Rachel down, as Rachel was shaking uncontrollably, the adrenaline surging through her body in the aftermath of the attack. Lucretia handed Rachel a drink.

"Vodka, it will steady nerves," she said.

"Thank you." Rachel took the shot and swallowed it in one go. As the heat of the vodka reached the back of her throat, it made her cough, but it soothed her at the same time. "That hit the spot!"

"Another?" Lucretia asked.

Rachel nodded and did the same again. The trembling was settling and her emotions were back in check.

"Sorry for disturbing you, but I couldn't let him go to use the telephone," she explained.

"Did he try to rape?" Lucretia asked, putting her arm around Rachel. Rachel appreciated the woman's concern, but wasn't sure how much to say, not wanting them to know she was a police officer in case Asimov was involved in Jefgeny's disappearance.

"I'd rather not talk about it. Thank you so much for your help. I'd better get back to my room now until the chief of security comes."

"I understand." Lucretia spoke softly. "Vladimir will escort you safe to room." She nudged the confused looking Asimov.

"Yes, of course. Where is your room?"

Rachel smiled. "It's the suite opposite yours."

"Oh! Well come along then." He led her across the rear corridor, back to the safety of her room. She swiped the card in the door and he noticed the mess inside where the fight had taken place. "Looks like you need Mario. Shall I call for him?"

"No, thank you. I'll deal with it later."

"Where you learn to fight?" he asked with admiration in his voice.

"I'm a karate black belt." Rachel decided not to mention additional self defence from the police academy. He seemed satisfied with the answer.

Seeing the weapon lying on the floor, he said, "If I were you, or if it had happened to Lucretia, I would have used knife." He pivoted and strode back to his room. Rachel saw Lucretia waiting in the doorway and waved before closing the door.

Rachel had showered, dressed and made a cup of coffee by the time Waverley knocked on her door. She presumed he would have a universal door swipe, so called out.

"Come in."

Her whole body was weak and jelly like. She reasoned this was as a result of the adrenaline release, the fight and lack of sleep.

Waverley looked worried when he caught sight of her and squeezed her shoulder before sitting down opposite. "How are you?"

"I've been better." She forced a smile.

He was taking in the surroundings and looking at the knife on the floor.

"I haven't touched it. It's evidence. You'll need to fingerprint it, and won't find any of mine on it." Rachel's emotions had shut down; she was speaking on autopilot.

Waverley appeared relieved. "That's good. Please can you tell me what happened here?"

Rachel explained how she couldn't get to sleep and how, on hearing someone trying to get into her room, she'd surprised them.

"He seemed like a drunk, to be honest, but I was stupid because a drunk wouldn't have a key card to my room, and this man did."

"How did that happen?"

"I lost mine yesterday – I realise now it was him who bumped into me, knocking my bag out of my hands. The contents spilled out. He helped me pick them up, which must have been when he took the key. I assumed I'd lost it, and as they don't have room numbers or names on them, I thought it would be okay. I also double-lock at night, but I was tired and not thinking straight when I opened the door."

"Do you know this man?"

"No, I don't. He's the brother of someone I recently arrested for murder, so there was a resemblance. I received a threatening letter after the trial, but didn't take it too seriously. He said his brother sent his regards when he held the knife to my throat."

"What was the brother's name?" asked Waverley, taking notes.

"Tansley – Steven Tansley."

"That confirms it – the man's name is Ray Tansley. He'll be locked up now for the rest of the cruise and we'll hand him over to the police in New York. I need to bag up the knife. If you don't mind, I'll send someone to come and fingerprint the door and the key card he used to get in. Were you in one of the public areas when he bumped into you?"

"Yes, I was in the main atrium on my way to meet Sarah. It was just before three."

"We'll look at video footage from that time. We should have enough evidence, along with the knife and your testimony, to put him away for attempted murder, or at least aggravated assault. I need to ask you to drop in to see Dr Bentley later this morning. He'll write a full report of the injuries and take photos. I'll let him know to expect you. Is that alright? I can ask him to visit you here if you prefer."

"No, let your team come and gather any evidence they need. His fingerprints will be on the curtain and the balcony door. He was going to throw me overboard."

She grimaced. The irony was not lost on Waverley, who scowled.

"I'll let Dr Bentley know to expect you first thing. The perpetrator denies attacking you, says you invited him up to your room, but we have enough evidence to keep him locked up for the duration. With forensics as well, he won't get away with it. My team are searching his room as we speak and I suspect there will be more evidence to find there. He will not bother you again, Rachel." Waverley used her first name in a fatherly manner, which she appreciated.

"Thank you."

Rachel took a deep breath, relieved that she had escaped with her life again. Working as cruise ship security sounded pretty good to her right now.

Waverley got up. "Mario will ensure your room gets a thorough clean up once my team have finished. I suggest you stay away for a few hours this morning. I'll send them up around 8am, if that suits?"

Rachel looked at the time: 5am. "Yes, that will be fine."

Waverley left, and Rachel crashed out like a light in the chair where she sat.

Chapter 28

Chief of security, Jack Waverley, who stood at six foot four, prided himself on being physically fit for a fifty-six year old. He looked in the mirror back in his stateroom after taking a shave. Apart from carrying an extra stone, brought about by the attentions of Monique, a senior cook in the bakery with whom he was having a relationship, he looked good.

He liked his work the *Coral Queen*. It certainly beat the stress of working in the military police for the navy, where he had been a petty officer for twenty years. This cruise, though, was proving challenging, and he had a lot on his mind.

Before being called to Rachel Prince's room, he had been worrying she might be right about Jefgeny Popov hiding somewhere aboard ship. He still hoped his hypothesis about Popov killing his friend, Erik Marinov, would turn out to be true, but he had growing doubts having questioned the engineering crew further. They all confirmed Erik had protected Popov. On top of that, there was the quandary over where Jefgeny would get a syringe, needle and drugs that would kill the big man.

The more he thought about it, the more doubts he had, which left him with a thumping headache. Could one of the other crew members be responsible, and if so, who? As far as Waverley could work out, Erik had had no enemies. He'd worked hard and, unlike many of the crew, hadn't drunk very much, preferring to study engineering books in his spare time.

Jefgeny Popov was more of a mystery – kept himself to himself, spoke only in Russian (even though he must have spoken English, being a US citizen), but he also worked hard, and going AWOL was totally out of character according to Steve Rafferty, the engineering chief. Jefgeny's only weakness appeared to be the demon drink. His colleagues said he could hold his alcohol, and despite being able to drink more than most, he had never appeared drunk.

Waverley had been going through the case in his head, having informed Captain Jenson of Rachel's suspicions and got his agreement to have Jefgeny's girlfriend watched.

"Do what you have to do, but for pity's sake, don't let any harm come to the passengers," Captain Jensen had said. "Are we certain the Russian passenger died from natural causes?"

Waverley had answered cautiously. "As far as the medical team can tell, he died of a heart attack or an overdose. There is the empty pill box found in the room—"

"Found by Miss Prince, again. She seems to have a knack for being in the thick of things, and was one of the last people to see Popov before he went missing."

"You're not suggesting she had anything to do with it?"

"No – of course not! It's just a pity she's a passenger, rather than on your team – she seems such a bright young thing, and could be useful to you, but she *is* a passenger."

Waverley heard the veiled warning to curb her involvement. "Yes, sir. I don't see any need to involve her further, and Miss Prince has assured me that her only wish is to enjoy her cruise and go shopping in New York."

"Good – we can't have passengers put in danger – no matter how useful they might be."

The pressure had mounted – Waverley needed to solve the murder of Erik

Marinov and find out what had happened to Jefgeny Popov, but his main priority was to protect the rest of the passengers and crew. He had been just about to fall asleep when his radio sparked into life, informing him of the attack on Rachel Prince. He couldn't believe it.

He returned to his room only too aware that this lovely young woman had almost been killed on his watch. Waverley was not a man prone to self-doubt, but even he wondered if he might be losing his edge. He looked again at his tired reflection in the mirror. This shouldn't be happening to him.

After shaving, he changed into his day uniform and marched into the main security station. As he entered, Ravanos and Brody stood to attention.

"It's okay, boys, be seated. Is our man securely locked away?"

"Yes, sir," answered Ravanos.

"Anything else to report overnight?"

"Not really," said Brody. "A rowdy group in the disco, but they didn't give us any trouble when we suggested they call it a night. One elderly man reported his watch stolen, but has just phoned to say he found it in his dress suit. We've got no further with the supposed jewellery theft."

Brody looked sceptical. Waverley knew about the case – a middle-aged passenger called Mrs Munro appeared to be the constant victim of jewellery thefts over several cruises.

"We'll leave that one to the insurance company, but keep up the pretence of looking for the missing jewellery."

"Sorry we had to wake you, sir," said Ravanos. "We knew you'd want to be informed of such a severe attack on Miss Prince."

"That's why I'm here. I need you to pull up security footage from the main atrium: timeline 2.30 to 3.30pm yesterday. Miss Prince says the man may have been someone who bumped into her deliberately and stole her room key card."

They carried out the laborious task of scrolling through video footage from different cameras, but it eventually yielded results.

"Stop there! That's Miss Prince. Scroll through slowly," Waverley instructed.

"There, sir." Brody pointed to a man bumping into her.

"Okay, scroll back and play it slowly. Yes, that looks deliberate. There, watch his left hand as he helps her pick up things with his right."

Sure enough, they saw him pick up the key card and slip it into his pocket before excusing himself and walking away.

"We only have a rear view – he's heading towards the shops. Pull the video from that area."

Eventually they found what they were looking for and identified Ray Tansley as the man who had bumped into Rachel.

"Gotcha," said Waverley happily. "Make copies of these so we can hand them over to the police in New York, and to the British police. The time has come for me to interview Mr Ray Tansley."

Waverley marched off with a spring in his step. Maybe his luck was changing.

Waverley arrived at the brig where the prisoner was being held and asked the officer on guard to bring the man to a small room nearby for questioning. Tansley came into the room wearing handcuffs and stared hard at Waverley. Thirty years old, the ship record had stated.

Waverley summed up the man in front of him. Six foot tall, rotund with cold eyes and tattoos lining muscular arms, he had a few bruises to his face and arms and a gash to the back of his head. Dr Romano had glued the gash together. A tough looking hooligan, Waverley concluded.

"What am I doing here? You've no right to lock me up. I'm the one that's been attacked by a loony woman. After inviting me up to her room, she turned demented."

"Really, and why would this woman attack you, Mr Tansley?"

"She obviously got cold feet. One minute, she gave me the come-on, the next minute she behaved like I was trying to rape her. You know what girls like that are like."

Tansley leered. Waverley gripped the pen in his hand, resisting the urge to punch the low-life in front of him. He had dealt with men like this all his life and found himself becoming less tolerant as he got older. He was pleased to see Rachel had inflicted some damage, and that alone consoled him. He marvelled at her resilience and the skill she must possess to disarm a man this size, punching well above her weight.

"I assume the knife in her room belonged to her, then?"

"Well, it's not mine, is it? What's more, I want to press charges against her."

"Please take a seat, Mr Tansley."

"My friends call me Ray." Tansley smirked.

I'd like to wipe that grin off your face. Waverley felt rage, but remained the picture of self-control as he spoke.

"Let me tell you where we're at, *Mr Tansley*. You are under arrest for the attack and attempted murder of a passenger on board this ship."

Tansley protested, but Waverley continued.

"We've recovered the knife as evidence, and as Ms Prince did not touch it, we are certain the only fingerprints to be found on it will be yours."

"So I carry a knife, but that's not enough to charge me. You can only charge me with carrying an offensive weapon."

"You appear to know the law, Mr Tansley. However, we also have CCTV footage of you deliberately bumping into Ms Prince yesterday and stealing her room key. With her testimony and your motive, I can assure you that you will be charged. We know you're the brother of someone she testified against and who later threatened her.

"Trust me, Mr Tansley, you will remain locked away in our padded cell for the next few days. After that, you will be handed over to the authorities in New York and will be locked away there. You are likely to be deported back to the United Kingdom for charges there. Either way, you will not be allowed any freedom on board this ship or on US soil. Personally, I hope they lock you up and throw away the key. Goodbye, *Mr Tansley*, I trust you will have a pleasant sailing aboard the *Coral Queen*."

Tansley shouted and cursed while being escorted back to the brig. Waverley walked away, punching the air, pleased with life.

Now, back to the Popov case.

Chapter 29

Hammering on the door roused Rachel from a deep sleep. After dragging herself up from the sofa and answering, she was greeted by two security guards.

"Sorry to disturb you, ma'am. We can come back later if you prefer?"

"No, now will be fine. Just give me five minutes and I'll leave you to it." Rachel rinsed the sleep out of her eyes and brushed her hair through before grabbing her handbag and leaving. She waved good morning to Mario, who was coming out of Asimov's room, drawing a concerned look as he shook his head in disbelief and blew her a kiss. She smiled weakly and headed upstairs.

The buffet was buzzing with people enjoying their holidays and filling up with as much food as they could eat before going about their recreational activities. Rachel felt envious, having had a stark reminder of the dangers of her day job.

Why, oh why did I get myself involved in another investigation? What's worse, I forgot about my night-time sortie in the depths of the ship when I spoke to Waverley this morning. Not that it would have been a good time to broach the subject. Now he won't let me have anything to do with the Jefgeny case, I've no idea how to keep Sarah out of it.

Her head hurt and her muscles ached.

After wandering around the buffet for about ten minutes, she finally filled a bowl with fresh fruit. The endless buffet options were too much for her today and the choice overwhelmed her.

She found a quiet place to sit. The welcome sound of her Jamaican friend singing as he pushed a trolley laden with hot drinks reminded her that all was normal.

"Good morning to my favourite lady. What can I get you this morning?"

"Strong coffee, please."

He poured the drink and moved along, not noticing, or choosing not to notice, the scratches to her neck. She had pulled on a polo shirt earlier and wore the collar up, but the marks had still been visible when she'd checked in the mirror. Her arms ached from the exertion of pinning Tansley's arm behind his back for so long – it had taken all her strength, powered by the will to live, to hold him in a vice-like grip, and her biceps were shouting about it.

Before she got up to leave, Thomas rushed over to her, his face filled with concern. He embraced her.

"I heard what happened last night. I'm so sorry – did he hurt you? Oh, your neck! Is that a bruise on your face?"

Rachel had to smile at how the words tumbled out of his mouth. He looked worried as he took a seat opposite.

"Thomas, calm down – I'm alright. Look, I'll tell you what's been going on, but you must promise not to tell anyone else – especially not any of the Russian tour party."

"I promise," he said, adding a cross my heart motion for good measure.

"Drinks?" Rachel's Jamaican friend returned with the trolley.

"More coffee for me, please," said Rachel.

"Tea with two sugars," said Thomas.

Once Rachel was satisfied that nobody else in the vicinity was in earshot or listening, she started.

"The man who attacked me last night is the brother of someone I got put away for murder. I work in Leeds as a policewoman and I witnessed a stabbing. After the trial, I received a threatening letter, and last night was an attempt at vengeance. The man would have thrown me overboard if I hadn't managed to turn things around. I didn't tell Asimov or Lucretia the full story because there's something else going on, and it might involve one of your tour party. I don't want them to know I'm a policewoman."

Thomas was a good listener and Rachel found it cathartic, talking to someone about the Tansley incident and his brother turning up last night.

"Well, you're a dark horse, I must say. I had you down as a model or a film star," he said, winking. "Are you going to tell me about the other thing then?"

"Perhaps later. I need to see the doctor so he can write a report of my injuries to go with the knife and other evidence from the attack last night."

Thomas's eyes widened. "Knife? OMG, Rachel!"

"I know, it was super scary, but at least he's locked up now."

"Good job – I'd like to get my hands on him even though I'm a pacifist. Where is he?"

"In the brig."

"Oh, I didn't think about that. I guess they must have a lock-up on board a ship this size."

"You'd be surprised what they've got on board this ship, Thomas," she teased as she got up. "I'll catch you later."

As soon as Rachel arrived at the medical centre, Sarah came rushing out.

"They told me what happened. Oh Rachel, I'm so relieved you're safe." They hugged each other as Dr Bentley came out of his surgery.

"Why don't you both come in while I examine Rachel – if you don't mind, Rachel?"

"I'd love to have Sarah with me. Thank you."

They followed Dr Bentley into surgery, and after offering his condolences and support, he took a full history of the events of the night before. He examined Rachel, writing notes and using a tape measure to measure the size of the scratches and bruises. Dr Bentley then took several photos after asking Rachel's permission and uploaded them on to his computer.

He asked her if there had been any attempt at sexual assault. She assured him that her attacker had only had one goal, and that was to kill her in revenge for putting his brother behind bars.

"That's all I need from an evidence perspective. I'm sorry someone has attacked you on board a Queen Cruise again, though."

"This man would have attacked me wherever – he obviously supposed a cruise ship to be an ideal place for murder. I'm just pleased he didn't stab me first, but I guess it would have been too messy."

"Rachel, don't – it makes me shudder at the thought of how much danger you were in," pleaded Sarah.

"Sorry, but it's over and he's behind bars."

"Not quite bars on a ship, but we get the gist." Dr Bentley turned away from his computer and Rachel sensed he wanted to say something else. She looked at him. "While you're both here – I know it might not be a good time, Rachel, but I need to get something off my chest."

"What is it, Graham?" asked Sarah.

"It's this Marinov and Popov business – I'm sure you've not let it go, Rachel, which is why I want to go over some things that are bothering me."

Rachel looked sheepish. "What things?"

"The injection, for a start – we are so strict about drugs and crew members undergo regular screening. Neither had any history of drug abuse, so if Marinov's death involved Popov – where did he get a syringe, needle and the wherewithal to kill his friend? Killing in this way would be premeditated, which doesn't fit in with a heat of the moment kind of killing."

Dr Bentley seemed relieved to get his thoughts out in the open, and Rachel couldn't have agreed more. "We've both had doubts, and you have just confirmed what we've been thinking: that Jefgeny did not kill Erik Marinov. We also suspect he's hiding on board the ship and that his girlfriend, Eva Sipka, is helping him."

"What makes you think that, and if he is innocent, why doesn't he just come forward?"

Rachel didn't want to mention what they had discovered last night because she didn't want to get Sarah into trouble. She was not good at lying and so she didn't speak for a while.

"Rachel spoke to his girlfriend, and she gave away little titbits of information that suggested Jefgeny is still alive," said Sarah.

"We need to tell Waverley."

"Already done," said Rachel. "He is having her watched and will pull her in before we get to New York if they don't find him by then."

"I still don't understand why he's hiding."

"Perhaps he doesn't trust the authorities, or maybe he has some other reason," offered Rachel. Keeping information from this kind and distinguished man didn't sit comfortably, but protecting Sarah's job came first. Sarah was also looking guilty, so Rachel took a different tack. "If you don't suspect Jefgeny – do you have another theory?"

"Not really – it would need to be someone who has access to syringes and needles and medication that can kill. There might be an illicit drugs racket on board, and if Erik found out about it, someone might have killed him to keep him quiet."

Rachel had to admit there was logic in the theory. "I hadn't thought of that, but that would explain the suddenness of the murder and the attempt at subterfuge. Perhaps Jefgeny knows about it too and that's why he's hiding. You said security carry regular tests out on crew?"

"They do, but if it's smuggling rather than drug taking, that's more complicated. We've got good security, but there are ways for the ultra-determined to get things on board a ship this size. I'll talk to Waverley and see if we can get some sniffer dogs on board when we call in at New York. In the meantime, I suggest you have a relaxing day at sea, Rachel."

"That's a great idea on both counts," said Sarah, pleased.

"Yes, agreed," said Rachel.

Dr Bentley was almost joyful having talked the matter through, as if someone had lifted a great weight from his shoulders.

Chapter 30

There was work to be done – first on her list was Thomas. Rachel pulled the dog eared Russian itinerary from her handbag and studied it to determine the best place to track him down. After running a finger through the list of activities, she spotted a talk being hosted by one of the guest speakers entitled *Russian Art – influences past and present*. Thomas's initials were next to the session. The talk started at 11am so she had time to return to her room to see if there was an internet signal, her near-miss last night still preying on her mind.

Rachel felt much calmer having received an email from Carlos and was ready to continue her investigation. She hadn't mentioned the early morning encounter with Ray Tansley because she didn't want him stressing out about her. His email had been chipper and mentioned he'd resolved his recent issue and was now working a different case. She wished someone would solve her complex case – maybe it was a drug smuggling racket as Dr Bentley suggested. In that case, she would not need to tell Waverley about her excursion below the waterline last night.

Rachel arrived early at the Plato lounge near to the Queen Art Gallery on deck six and took a seat. One of the crew was demonstrating the operation of a handheld remote to the guest speaker, who carried out a few sound and visual checks. She heard Asimov's voice as he entered the room with around twenty of the group. Lucretia was with him and she walked over to Rachel.

"How are you?"

"I'm much better now that man's locked away. Thank you for your help last night, I'm sorry I disturbed you."

"That was not a problem. I am light sleeper and Vladimir was happy to help damsel in distress. His bite is worse than his bark."

Rachel smiled at the misquote but appreciated the sentiment.

"Lulu," Asimov was calling for Lucretia to take her seat beside him.

"I'd better go. He doesn't like art, he is more technical man, but I love, so he comes with me."

Lucretia joined Asimov and he nodded to Rachel, not giving much away, but at least it was an acknowledgement. Rachel saw Boris in the group along with the tall grey-haired man called Sergei.

Thomas arrived armed with the clipboard and ticked off his list of attendees before spotting Rachel. As soon as he did, he joined her.

"My day has just got better." He flirted for effect in front of his Russian audience. Rachel smiled, and then he put on a brief act of seeing her scratches for the first time before whispering, "I'm free after this session if you want to talk."

"Yes, that would be fine. I have something to show you," she whispered back.

The speaker introduced himself as Mishka Orlov, a lecturer from the University of Pennsylvania, specialising in the history of art, and in particular, Russian artists. He was a natural orator who held the audience's attention for forty-five minutes; even Asimov looked as though he was enjoying himself, laughing at Mishka's jokes and listening intently. After a fifteen minute question time at the end of his talk, Mishka managed a quick plug of his latest book, with the same title as the talk, holding up a copy. He had several copies with him –

books he offered to sign. Otherwise, the book was on sale in Coral Bookshop on deck five. Almost everyone attending bought a copy at $49.00 each, and a crew member was on site to swipe their onboard payment cards.

Rachel and Thomas left. "Where would you like to lunch?" Thomas asked.

"Are you happy with the grill? I feel like taking on some fat after my exertions last night."

"Suits me, let's go." Thomas took her arm, and they headed up to deck fourteen.

Once they'd stocked up with food, they found a table and chatted while they ate.

"He was a surprisingly good speaker – I thought the talk would be dry," remarked Thomas.

"I only attended to meet up with you, but I really enjoyed it," agreed Rachel. "If I imagined I might ever open a page of his book, he would have tempted me to buy one too."

"Yes, his talk did the selling for him, didn't it? I gather Lucretia loves that sort of thing. She drags Mr Asimov around all the art galleries. He's bought her a few special pieces too, apparently."

"Looks like a man in love, and she has a good influence on him," said Rachel. "It's a shame he can't lose that scowl."

"Men with money don't have to pretend, I guess," replied Thomas. "He doesn't seem to care whether people like him, and I hear he has a foul temper. It wouldn't surprise me if he was involved in some dirty dealings. Boris doesn't seem to like him at all, and the rest of the group are on the payroll in one way or another, from what I can gather."

"What about the women?"

"Wives, girlfriends or paid escorts – just having a good time at Asimov's expense. He has money to burn."

"Are you any wiser on where Sergei fits in?"

"Sergei Markov? I still can't work it out, other than his shared business interests with Mr Asimov – he isn't on the payroll and keeps himself to himself. It wouldn't surprise me if he was some sort of covert business manager or negotiator. He has some health problems too, from what I understand – he's diabetic. One of the nurse's has to keep supplying him with insulin, which is annoying the doctor."

"What makes you think he's a covert business manager?"

"No particular reason, except he and Mr Asimov have private meetings that not even Lucretia attends."

"How do you know?"

"Because they use my room when they want to talk in private."

"That is interesting," said Rachel.

They finished eating and Rachel studied Thomas. Deciding to trust him, she took her phone out of her handbag and scrolled through to the photos she had taken the night before.

"Thomas, do you read Russian as well as speak the language?"

"I'm familiar with the alphabet so can make out most words, why?"

"Take a look at the writing on this picture. Can you make out what it says?" Rachel handed him the phone.

Thomas used two fingers to enlarge the photo to help him focus and took reading glasses out of his shirt pocket. "Let me see, the first word is easy. It says *me*. Okay, the next word is *with*, then *Bianca*. I take it the writing is off the back of a photo?"

"Carry on," prompted Rachel.

Thomas looked at the photo again. "*And* is the next word, then a capital B, followed by o, r, i... OMG, it says *Boris*! Do you have the photo?"

Rachel, not sure how much she trusted Thomas, evaded the question. "What does the rest say?"

"Hm, it's a place name. Oh, that's easy, it says *St Petersburg 1999*."

Rachel put her hand out for the phone and, scrolling to the photo, she zoomed in on the second man. Yes, it could be Boris Stanislav, but it was hard to be certain. Taking the plunge, she passed the phone back to Thomas.

"What do you think of this?" she said.

"The man on the right looks familiar. It might be Boris Stanislav, but it's quite faded, and the beard and moustache make it difficult to say. I'm not sure. Boris is a common name in Russia. Where did you get the photo and why is it important?" Thomas looked as if he was enjoying himself.

"I can't tell you that, Thomas." He looked deflated. "But you could do something for me, if you don't mind."

His eyes lit up. "Ooh, yes please. I love a bit of detective work."

"Can you get to speak with Boris? I'm sure he's hiding something, and the issue with the minders makes me suspect Asimov is having him watched. It might be nothing."

"I'll try. He likes cards, so I can take him to the casino tonight and see what I can find out. I'll ply him with drinks." Thomas rubbed his hands together, excited.

"Be careful, Thomas. I'm not sure what's going on, but it might be dangerous. Whatever you do, keep it natural. Also, try to get some information about his family. He has a wife and two sons, but does he have a sister or brother, and are they married?"

"You think that's Boris in the photo, don't you?"

"I'm not certain."

Thomas looked at his watch. "Time to go, I'm afraid. Golf simulation with some of the ladies!" He rolled his eyes.

Rachel smiled at him. "Make sure you flirt madly."

He laughed as he walked away.

Rachel hoped she had done the right thing involving him, but he was her closest link to the group, and the only one she could trust. Natalia was the other one who might help, but it was best to proceed cautiously. Another idea was developing in her head, but it would take some careful planning and she might need help.

Chapter 31

Guilt weighed heavily on Sarah's mind. She was not happy at concealing her foray into Jefgeny's room last night, and now Rachel had been assaulted. Worry for her friend whipped her head into a frenzy. *What if she puts herself in danger again?* There was only one thing for it and that was to see Waverley herself and confess. If it meant losing her job, so be it. At least Rachel would be safe.

The initial euphoria over Graham's theory had worn off. Although there might be some truth in it, for her it made no sense. It was ludicrous to envisage a drug smuggling cartel operating in secret below decks. Also, knowing Rachel would not stop and might end up dead worried her silly.

Two bodies are quite enough for one cruise.

Resigning herself to her fate, she finished morning surgery on autopilot.

Bernard popped his head through the door. "Hey, have you finished? We can go get lunch if you're free?"

"That would be good. Will anyone else be coming? I can't face eating with Lauren today."

"Nope, just you and me. Lauren's gone with Graham to read the riot act to the Russian guy who keeps mislaying his insulin. Alex is finishing up, then going for a sleep after being up all night again, and Gwen is catching up with paperwork and billing."

"In that case, let's go." She powered down the computer.

"Can we eat in the officers' dining room? You never know when we'll get to eat a proper meal again. You're on call tonight." They usually ate in the buffet, but occasionally indulged in a bigger meal at lunchtime to stock up in case they missed an evening meal.

"That's fine. I just need to sign out the glue I used to fix a laceration before we go."

The storage room where they kept supplies and medicines locked away was neat as ever. Sarah filled in the logbook. "Looks like Lauren's been busy. She's signed out more meds than any of us."

"Might have been from the cardiac arrest – she did all the paperwork. And the poor girl has to keep supplying the Russian guy with insulin."

"Oh yes, I forgot about that. The cardiac arrest seems an age ago, but it was only yesterday, wasn't it?"

"I know what you mean. Come on, Sarah. I'm starving."

Sarah closed the book. "You're always starving. Be careful – your wife won't recognise you if the Michelin Man comes home."

"The Michelin Man?"

Sarah explained about an advert for tyres and the accompanying round Michelin Man, trademarked by a tyre company. "You need to spend time in the UK."

"And when might I do that? My whole life's spent on this ship, and in between I need to get home to see my family."

"I tell you what, let's see if we can swing it to take a day off when we dock in Southampton and do the London trip. I would love to show you round London."

"Wow, Nurse Bradshaw, you're on. It's a date."

"Better not mention it to Lauren, or I might find cyanide in my tea!"

Bernard nudged her as they made their way to the officers' dining room for lunch. "Hopefully she got the message loud and clear," he muttered.

Sarah enjoyed eating in the officers' dining room sometimes because it was waiter service with a full menu, not dissimilar to the one the passengers chose from. During her nursing training, she'd learned not to let stress affect her appetite or she would have starved long ago, stress being a nurse's lot.

One of the waiters, an Indian man called Rai, bantered with Bernard for a little while before taking their order. It always amazed her how many people Bernard knew on board; he had a gift for remembering names.

"I'll have pâté followed by a rack of lamb," said Bernard.

"And for you, miss?" asked Rai.

"Shrimp cocktail and chicken with basil, please."

Bernard poured them both some water. "What's on your mind, Sarah? I can tell you're worried about something."

"I'm concerned about Rachel more than anything. She seems to attract trouble these days."

"She sure does. Someone told me about the attack last night, but she's alright now, isn't she?"

"Hopefully," said Sarah. "It's been a depressing few days with the two deaths; I'll be glad to get to New York."

"Three deaths, more like, as your Mr Popov is probably shark bait somewhere."

"Bernard, that's horrible! Anyway, Rachel's not sure he is. She's convinced he's somewhere on board and hiding. Graham's now thinking along those lines too."

"So you're worried Rachel will get herself in some sticky situation again?"

Sarah nodded.

"She's a big girl, and from what I understand of last night, she can take care of herself. Don't worry, she'll probably get to the bottom of it like a young *Miss*

Marple and then tell the chief of security whodunit."

Sarah laughed. "You've heard of *Miss Marple* then?"

"Oh yes, my wife loves those books, reads them all the time. We watched the series together on satellite television. We're not completely backward in the Philippines, you know."

"I never thought you were." She was about to apologise when she noticed the teasing glint in his eye. "How does your wife put up with you?"

"Why do you think she sends me away to work?"

They finished their meal and Bernard returned to the medical centre to collect the on-call bag for the afternoon. Sarah accompanied him, putting off her visit to Waverley's office for a while.

When they arrived back, Gwen was not in her office. There were sounds of a commotion coming from the infirmary.

Walking in, they found Graham, Gwen and Lauren treating a young woman. Alex arrived almost immediately afterwards.

"What happened?" he asked, looking concerned.

"She collapsed in the casino," said Graham. "It doesn't appear to be anything serious, but she looks anaemic. Working too hard, I suspect."

"It's Eva Sipka, the girlfriend of the missing crewman. She's twelve weeks pregnant," said Alex.

"Oh," said Graham. "There's no blood loss and no abdominal pain, but perhaps we'll keep her in overnight just to be on the safe side."

Sarah groaned. "That's the end of my afternoon off."

"I'll look after her," Lauren piped up, looking gooey eyed at Alex.

Talk about Jekyll and Hyde!

"Thank you, Lauren. You get some rest, Sarah," said Alex kindly.

"Okay, I'm not complaining. I'll be back later to collect the on-call kit."

Sarah left the medical centre, pondering the weird girl that was Lauren. *One minute she's Cruella Deville, the next minute, Florence blooming Nightingale. I really can't work her out. I expect there's some ulterior motive. She must fancy Alex now Bernard's out of bounds – astonishing.*

Sarah approached Waverley's office, half hoping he wouldn't be there, but he was. She knocked on the door. He looked up from his desk and beckoned her in, looking weary.

"Nurse Bradshaw. What can I do for you – is Rachel alright?"

"I assume so, I haven't seen her since this morning. Has Dr Bentley been to see you?"

"Yes, he has." His tone sharpened. "He told me his ridiculous drug smuggling theory, and quite honestly, it's inconceivable we could have criminal activity of that level going on under our noses. Our security is rigorous, it's not possible. I'm sorry to disappoint, but I don't accept for one minute this is the case. I do wish people would stop playing amateur detective and leave me to get on with my work. I don't tell him how to do his job, do I?"

Sarah suspected this would not be a good time to confess her crime or she could end up sharing a cell with Ray Tansley.

"Oh well, if you're sure."

"Was that what you were here about?"

"Yes, sir. Sorry, I didn't mean to interrupt your work."

Sarah headed towards the door and Waverley followed her. "Look, Nurse Bradshaw – Sarah – I'm sorry for being short. It's been a long day and I still have a missing man who may or may not be on board. I'm going to speak to his girlfriend, despite what Rachel Prince might say. It's time to put this case to bed."

"I'm sorry, but Eva Sipka's taken ill. She passed out at work and is in the infirmary," said Sarah.

"GREAT! That's all I need. How long will she be there?"

"At least overnight," Sarah answered and walked away, sighing. She had a funny feeling Waverley's day was not going to get any better.

Oh well, at least I still have a job for now.

Chapter 32

On her way to Waverley's office, Rachel saw Sarah walking towards her.

"Hi, where are you heading?" asked Sarah.

"I'm going to see Waverley to discuss Jefgeny Popov."

"Not a good time – you're likely to get your head bitten off, even if you are a passenger. I've just been, but before I got the chance to confess about last night, he read me the riot act and told me in no uncertain terms to leave any investigating to him. He's annoyed about Graham getting involved."

"Blast, that's not what I wanted to hear."

"He's tired and stressed by all the trouble he's had to deal with. He'll calm down later. Why don't we get afternoon tea and then you can walk me back to the medical centre?"

"That sounds like a great idea." Rachel linked arms with Sarah and they made their way to their favourite haunt, Creams.

After ordering, Rachel explained what she'd found out from Thomas over lunch: how it seemed that Boris was related to or friends with Jefgeny.

"Do you think it is your Boris?"

"He's not *my* Boris, but I'm pretty sure it is. It would explain why Jefgeny tried to speak to him that first day when they met in the corridor. If it is, it also suggests that Jefgeny might be hiding from Boris or Sergei Markov, because he's the other one that spoke to Jefgeny."

"We don't seem to be getting very far, and the drug idea seems far-fetched. Despite what Graham believes – and Waverley didn't hold truck with Graham's theory, by the way – the most likely explanation is still that Jefgeny killed his friend and is hiding or dead."

"But how did he inject him, and what is the connection to the Russian group?" asked Rachel.

"I don't know. Perhaps the injection mark is not that at all, or maybe Erik took an overdose."

"Possible, but no suicide note? It doesn't make sense."

"None of it makes sense, Rachel. I just want it to end so I don't have to worry about you roaming around on your own, putting yourself in danger."

"It's okay, I'm not on my own. I've got a recruit."

"Who? Don't tell me – Thomas?"

Rachel smiled at the concerned look on Sarah's face. "I'll be fine, and Thomas is only going to do a bit of listening in for me – nothing dangerous."

"I hope you're right, because if Waverley gets wind of this, we will both be in the doghouse. He's verging on apoplexy. The sooner we own up to what we did last night, the better."

"You said he's not in the mood for listening, so we'll just have to get on with it for now."

Sarah didn't look reassured, but at least she accepted things as they were.

They finished their tea, and Rachel walked Sarah back to the medical centre. When they got back, Bernard came rushing out to meet them.

"I'm glad you're here, Sarah. Lauren has gone missing and Graham's called me to help with a sick passenger on deck eleven. Alex is due any minute to check on Eva Sipka and Gwen's in her office, doing paperwork."

Sarah was livid. "I don't suppose you've told Gwen that Lauren is AWOL?"

He shook his head. "I daren't, she'll go mad." He turned and hurried away with the emergency case in tow.

Rachel looked concerned. "What's Eva Sipka doing here?"

"Sorry, I forgot to tell you, she fainted in the casino. She's fine – pregnant women can drop their blood pressure, and Alex suspects she's anaemic as well. She's in overnight. I wonder where that wretched woman is this time!"

Gwen came out of her office. "What wretched woman? Is everything alright?"

At that moment, Alex walked through the door and Sarah excused herself to accompany him for his examination of Eva. Rachel saw from Gwen's face that the situation was becoming clear.

She looked at Rachel.

"Where's Lauren?"

Rachel wasn't sure it was her place to say anything, so she shrugged her shoulders.

Sarah popped her head out of the infirmary. "Ms Sipka says Lauren's gone to her cabin to collect something for her."

"It's not good enough," muttered Gwen. "She can't just leave a patient unattended without telling me. That woman has no concept of ship hierarchy, thinks she can do as she pleases. Well I've had enough." Gwen wasn't as much speaking to Rachel as letting off steam. Sarah had gone back into the infirmary, and Rachel wasn't sure what to do.

"Can I get either of you some coffee?" Raggie appeared just in time.

"Yes please, Raggie. Rachel, do stay – I could do with a break. Come and join me."

Gwen motioned her to sit in one of three comfy chairs around a coffee table. There was also a two-seater settee, similar to the set up in Waverley's office. Rachel guessed senior officers had identical offices, and this one would be where Gwen's team held medical meetings.

"Sorry, Rachel, that was unprofessional of me. I trust you will use your discretion."

"My hearing's been playing up recently," Rachel replied, and they both laughed.

Gwen's computer pinged.

"Excuse me for one moment." Gwen moved over to the computer and tapped a few keys, her face paling.

"Are you okay?"

"Not really." She picked up the phone and spoke to whoever answered at the other end. "It's Sister Sumner, you need to come down here, now."

Rachel could tell this was something serious, but wasn't sure whether to go. "Should I leave you to it?" she asked, hoping Gwen would say no.

"You'd better, please, this is confidential. Have your coffee outside and see Sarah before you go, though."

Rachel was tempted to decline, but decided she might as well enjoy a percolated coffee.

She sat in the waiting room. Waverley burst through the doors, heading straight into Gwen's office, not noticing Rachel, whose radar was now on full alert.

What is Waverley doing here?

Raggie took coffee in to Gwen's office, but left the door ajar on his way out. He didn't spot Rachel either and left the centre, so she seized the opportunity and moved a chair closer to the office where she could listen in to what was being said.

"It sounded important, Sister. What is it?"

"Something's been bothering me about our new nurse. She seems to go missing far too often, and I noticed she's been signing out a lot of medication."

"Go on." Rachel detected from his tone that Waverley wanted the facts as quickly as possible.

"I pulled her CV and work history and realised she had worked at a hospital in Connecticut where I have a friend who is chief nurse. We go back a long way, but you don't want to know about that."

"Quite," said Waverley.

"Well, I decided to email her and ask if she knew anything about a Lauren Blythe who had worked there from 2006 to 2007. It was before her time, but she agreed to ask around. Emails have been a bit hit and miss over the past twenty-four hours, but I've just received one sent yesterday."

What does it say? Rachel had to stop herself saying it out loud.

"What does it say?" asked Waverley, sounding tense.

"It seems she left under a cloud. There were unsubstantiated rumours that drugs had been going missing from the ward."

"Are you telling me she might be a drug addict?"

"I wish it were that simple," Gwen answered. "The drug was insulin. Nothing was proven, but my friend has now interviewed all the nurses who worked there at that time, and they say in retrospect, there were a high number of patient deaths during her tenure."

Waverley gasped.

Gwen continued. "The thing is, none of them registered this in isolation, but now they all seem to say the same thing. My friend's predecessor encouraged Lauren Blythe to leave, feeling they didn't have enough evidence to call in the police. To cut a long story short, my friend has now involved the police who are looking into the deaths during that time period."

"Let me get this straight. You're telling me we might have a serial killer on board the *Coral*." Waverley's voice was shaking. "Are we sure it's the same nurse?"

"Certain. It prevented her from getting a job in a hospital again, according to my friend – mud sticks, but she got a job as an occupational health nurse at a company called Future Motors in Boston. She worked there until 2013, then moved to Africa."

Where have I heard that name before?

"NO!" Rachel couldn't stop herself shouting, which brought Waverley rushing out of Gwen's office.

"What the hell are you doing here?"

"Never mind that now. That company is where Jefgeny Popov worked until he reported some big players for industrial espionage. They tried to steal the prototype for a driverless car. Jefgeny ended up in witness protection. I suspect he saw her, and that's why he's in hiding. She knows who he is."

Sarah came out of the infirmary, picking up the last part of the sentence. "She was here after I'd seen him on the first day and took an interest in his record. I think she recognised him."

"You need to move quickly. She's gone down to Eva's room to get something. I'm sure that's where he's hiding," said Rachel.

"But even if you're right, why would she want to harm him?"

"I'm not sure yet, but she killed Erik Marinov with an insulin overdose, of that I'm certain."

"And Nikolai Stepanov," said Sarah as this new information dawned on her. "She was alone with him the night he died."

Waverley got on his radio. "Sarah, come with me. Sister, can you explain to Ms Sipka that her boyfriend might be in grave danger and ask her where he is hiding? Call me on the radio when you find out. Send Dr Bentley and Dr Romano after us

– we may need them. I'll ask you how you knew about the witness protection thing later, Miss Prince."

Sarah grabbed an emergency bag and followed Waverley.

"I'm coming too, Sarah might need help," said Rachel.

Waverley shrugged his shoulders in resignation and Rachel brought up the rear.

Chapter 33

Rachel could feel adrenaline pumping and anxiety building as they made their way through the private staff area and down several flights of stairs. Eva's room was on Deck B, two decks below the waterline. Waverley took the steps two at a time and Sarah pursued hard on his heels. Rachel's stilettos kept catching in the metal grids of the steps until she risked going barefoot and took them off.

By the time they got to deck B, Waverley was panting and had to stop. Rachel sympathised, but didn't slow down. Sarah raced on ahead and arrived at the room first with Rachel right behind.

Sarah unlocked Eva's door. Lauren looked surprised when they burst in. They saw a man lying on the floor; Rachel assumed him to be Jefgeny.

"Thank God," said Lauren. "I was just going to call for help. He collapsed; I think he might be dead."

"Get out of my way!" Sarah pushed past her and checked Jefgeny's vital signs. Lauren turned to assist.

"Oh, no you don't!" said Rachel, pulling her back and pinning her arms behind her back. At the same time, she checked Lauren's pockets and pulled out two medicine bottles.

"Let go of me! What are you doing?" Lauren shouted, at which point Waverley arrived, followed soon after by two security guards. He took control of the situation.

"Get her out of here," he ordered the security guards, who applied handcuffs to Lauren's wrists and marched her away.

"Is he alive?" asked Rachel, handing the bottles to Sarah so she could identify what Lauren had given the man.

"Barely."

Waverley shouted into his radio. "CODE BLUE. Doctors to deck B, 1932, I repeat—"

He didn't need to repeat the call as Dr Bentley and Bernard came running through the door.

"Was that Lauren I just saw in handcuffs?"

"It's a long story," answered Sarah. "Insulin overdose."

"Clear the area," ordered Dr Bentley. "Get a line in." Bernard handed Sarah the equipment to work with. "Glucagon injection," Dr Bentley commanded.

Bernard drew up the solution using a syringe and needle, and Graham injected it into Jefgeny's leg. Rachel moved out of the already cramped room and joined Waverley in the corridor while the medical team worked hurriedly, but efficiently. She hoped they were not too late.

"He's coming round," said Dr Bentley. "Right, team, let's get him on a stretcher and up to the infirmary. He's out of the woods."

"Will he survive?" asked Waverley.

"Yes," answered Dr Bentley. "She's used long and short acting insulin, but it's easy to reverse when you know what you're treating. We'll monitor his blood sugars and treat him accordingly. He has a sugar solution going in through the IV line, so all will be well."

Sarah and Bernard wheeled Jefgeny away and Dr Bentley followed. Waverley looked exhausted as he picked up his radio.

"Send fingerprinting equipment down, and seal the room for forensics – we'll need evidence." He turned to Rachel. "Perhaps you would like to accompany me to my office and explain what you know. I will see to Nurse Death later." His smile was grim.

"You'd better tell me the full story," said Waverley when they arrived at his office. He poured them both a glass of mineral water from a bottle out of his fridge. "When did you work out it was the nurse?"

"Only when I overheard your conversation with Gwen. I realised then it involved her, and it makes sense now because she would have access to the crew quarters while the Russian guests wouldn't. She also has access to medicines. Sarah said that one of the Russians kept losing his insulin – I suspect she was stealing it."

"What about the witness protection?"

"That's what Sarah and I wanted to confess today. We found out last night – don't blame Sarah, it was my fault." Rachel explained about their expedition downstairs the night before, and about finding the newspaper article and the photograph. "I'm still not sure of the relevance, although it seems that Jefgeny Popov and Boris Stanislav know each other. They may even be related. They must have recognised each other in the corridor when we took the tour of engineering."

"So has he been hiding from Mr Stanislav or Nurse Blythe?"

"The latter, I suspect, but he will answer that. She obviously recognised him from her time working at Future Motors. Perhaps she was involved in the initial conspiracy."

"That might be a leap too far, but it seems she's responsible for two deaths on board this ship, and one attempted murder. Case solved – looks like your Russians are innocent after all."

Rachel detected a hint of triumph in his voice and she couldn't blame him.

"I'm not sure all of them are innocent, but I grant you, they are not guilty of the murders."

"It's time for me to go to the medical centre to speak with Popov and his girlfriend. I suppose you want to tag along?"

"Yes please." She got up and followed before he could change his mind.

When they arrived at the medical centre, all appeared calm. Gwen escorted them through to the infirmary where Jefgeny was sitting up in the bed next to Eva. He looked tired and pale, but relieved.

"I need to ask you both some questions. Is that alright, Doctor Bentley?"

Doctor Bentley nodded tersely. "Don't be too long, we still need to run tests."

The pair looked frightened; both knew they would more than likely lose their jobs with the cruise line and not be able to work on board a ship again. Waverley pulled up two chairs and sat down, motioning for Rachel to do the same. He introduced Rachel, explaining that it was she they needed to thank that Jefgeny was alive. Realising the medical team were going nowhere, Waverley started his questioning.

"First, I need to ask you, Mr Popov, did you kill Erik Marinov?"

"No, sir, I did not."

"Do you know who did?"

"Not for sure, but I guess it was the nurse who tried to kill me."

"Why did you pretend that you couldn't speak English when I met you?" Sarah asked.

He looked at her. "I'm sorry, but since joining witness protection, I have trusted no-one."

"Who have you been hiding from?"

"I recognised man in Russian group. He was part of crime I reported before. They said they would never stop until they found us. My friend also went into protection. He is crazy – still visits Russia. I would never go again. I thought about coming to security, but these men have tentacles everywhere. When I decided to come to you later that day, I caught sight of the nurse in my room and thought I recognised her from the company, Fortune Motors. Terrified they had tracked me down and intended to kill me, I begged Eva to hide me – she no want to. She wanted me to come clean, but I was too afraid. It's not her fault."

"Never mind that now," said Waverley. "Where did you hide? We searched everywhere, including Miss Sipka's room."

"I hid in shaft above shower room. There is service hatch – engineers and electricians know these things. I hid there during day and with Eva at night."

"Does that mean your roommate knew of this, Miss Sipka?" Waverley asked.

"No, she works nights, so she did not know."

Rachel doubted that, but enough people would lose their jobs without adding to the tally.

"Is it Boris Stanislav you were hiding from?"

"No, he is my brother-in-law. We have not seen each other since I entered witness programme. He looked pleased and almost gave me away. Other man in the group may have recognised me, or maybe nurse was sent after me."

"Can you tell me the man's name?"

"No. I never met him, only saw from a distance. It's twenty years."

"It may have been a coincidence, Mr Popov. The woman seems to have been working alone; she even killed one of the Russians in the group. I'll show you photos of the men tomorrow to see if you can identify the man you recognised."

Jefgeny closed his eyes and Rachel noticed tears falling down his face. She couldn't be sure if they were tears of joy or sorrow.

"That's enough for now," Dr Bentley intervened. "Mr Popov needs time to recover. You can post a security guard down here if he's still in any danger."

"I don't think he is," answered Waverley. "But it can't do any harm. I'll send someone down. Perhaps you and I could get a drink later?" He looked at Dr Bentley.

"Yes, perhaps we will."

Sarah looked relieved that the spat between her two favourite men would be over soon.

"Good evening to you all. We will speak again tomorrow, Mr Popov. I will report to the captain. Murder case closed,

Miss Prince. Russian business transactions are no concern of ours."

Rachel took that to mean *butt out.*

"Yes, chief," she answered.

Day 5

Chapter 34

The next morning, Rachel decided to speak with Thomas during the day, and then forget about the whole thing. The nagging doubt at the back of her mind would have to go away. She'd been convinced one of the Russians was involved in the two deaths on board, in particular Asimov or the mysterious Sergei. It didn't make sense, though, as neither had any link to Lauren. Waverley's Russian friend had come up with nothing, and Waverley had told him to forget about it.

Maybe Lauren had acted alone, a psychopathic serial killer who used her nursing skills to exercise her need for control by deciding who should live and who should die. Rachel shuddered. She remembered reading about a doctor and pathological liar, Harold Shipman, who'd murdered hundreds of patients over decades before he was eventually found out. She had studied the interviews at the police training centre. The detectives interviewing him had said he'd mocked them – always believing his intellect was superior and they wouldn't be able to catch him out, he'd then been haughty even in court. Lauren had displayed some of that contempt to both her and Sarah, and she disregarded authority, so she fitted the bill. Rachel found it hard to comprehend.

Another example she remembered of a serial killer in the medical profession was a nurse called Beverley Allitt. *Didn't she use insulin too?* She'd murdered four children and attempted to murder more while working on a children's ward.

Yep, thankfully they're rare, but perhaps Lauren was one of the few. I dread to think how many she murdered in Africa. Rachel shuddered again.

Mario brought her a pot of coffee and she took it out to the balcony, happy there had been no stormy days or nights with only two more sea days to go before they arrived in New York.

The telephone rang.

"Hello."

"Rachel, it's Thomas. I've found out something, can we meet up?"

"Yes, when?"

"Can you come to my room, 1508, this afternoon about three? I'm chock-a-block with activities until then. I have something you should listen to."

Rachel wrote the room number down on a pad next to the telephone. "Okay, see you then."

After putting the telephone down, she wondered what Thomas had discovered. This could be the final piece in the puzzle.

Rachel knocked on the door of 1508 and Thomas answered immediately, looking breathless with excitement. Sweating profusely, he walked over to his safe and took out a digital recorder.

"I carry this everywhere. I keep a digital diary in case I ever want to write my memoirs," he explained, laughing.

He sat down on the sofa and Rachel took a seat next to him, intrigued.

"They are speaking in Russian so I'll need to interpret for you." He pressed play. "Tell me you had nothing to do with Nikolai Stepanov's death." Rachel recognised the voice of Asimov.

"He was blackmailing Boris." She assumed this was Sergei speaking, and Thomas confirmed this by mouthing, "Sergei."

There was silence for a moment. "I knew that, but it was in hand."

"It wasn't New York he found out about; it involved another matter. Not something that involves you."

"Astonishing! What other matter? I need to know about everything; I am taking big risk."

"It was nothing." Sergei sounded dismissive. "Boris had a brother-in-law who caused big trouble for us in the past. Nikolai discovered he was working on this ship. We planned to kill the man and didn't want Nikolai opening big mouth. We killed two birds with one stone."

"I don't believe what I'm hearing! You killed two men during this cruise? Unbelievable."

Thomas stopped the tape.

"They argue about it for a bit longer. Sergei explains that neither of the deaths could be linked to him; he has someone else on board who did the killings. I'll play and interpret the next bit, though, because it mentions that the wrong man was killed."

Thomas looked so pleased with himself, she didn't want to burst his bubble by telling him she already knew this.

Sergei spoke again and Thomas interpreted.

"We found out this man who took witness protection would be on this ship. We needed to get an accomplice on board to replace a crew member, so we arranged for a person's father to have an accident."

Rachel gasped – Brigitte's father had been an unwitting victim in this conspiracy.

"And this poor person's father – did you kill him too?"

"Of course not – he survived. He will recover. Anyway, we brought our accomplice on board and ran into some problems. They killed roommate by mistake after being caught in the man's room. Man we are looking for has killed himself – that's what accomplice says. Nikolai was greedy, and when he recognised Boris's brother-in-law, he threatened to expose him and get him killed – but I already knew about him."

Asimov took deep breaths before hissing, "Boris thinks I had something to do with Nikolai's death. Look, I signed up to do a favour for a friend, not to get involved with murder."

"I always hunt traitors down. Russia does not tolerate betrayal." Rachel could hear the edge in Sergei's voice and she almost felt sorry for Asimov.

"Is there not an investigation?"

"No, they have assumed the first death to be murder/suicide, and the second heart attack or overdose. We drugged Nikolai to mimic a heart attack."

"I haven't asked what is in the documents I expect Boris to collect because I don't want to know. Now I do want to know."

"The information they contain is worth billions of dollars, and one of your companies will get the contract to manufacture a state-of-the-art stealth aircraft like the world has never seen. Russia will be grateful to you, my friend."

Thomas stopped the recording again. "That's it – Asimov leaves the room after that."

"We need to take this to the security chief right now." Rachel stood up to go, but noticed Thomas remained where he was with his head in his hands. "What's wrong?"

"Rachel, I'm not sure about this. I'm not a brave man, and this Sergei Markov goes around killing people – I don't want to die."

Rachel saw he was trembling, with tears in his eyes.

"Look, I realise it's difficult, Thomas, but we can't let them get away with murder. Not only that, they intend to steal some pretty high-level security information."

"I'm really scared, Rachel – you need to give me more time to think about this. My schedule's full for the rest of the evening. Give me to tomorrow morning."

"Alright, but then I will need to tell the chief whether you come with me or not." Rachel was frustrated, but understood why Thomas was scared, and he had good reason to be. She offered up a quick prayer for Thomas, but she remained determined to see Markov arrested for his part in two murders.

"I'll be in the Twilight Room at 10am tomorrow for a treasure hunt. Meet me there. I don't want anyone to see you coming in here in case suspicions are raised."

"Can I take the recorder?"

"No, there's a lot of personal stuff on there from the cruise. I will need to make a copy of that first. You can have it tomorrow, with or without me. One more thing, Rachel. Promise me you won't tell anyone about this until after we've met tomorrow."

Rachel knew not to push him at this point or she might lose him.

"Okay, I promise."

She hoped she wouldn't come to regret her promise as she watched him return the recorder to his safe.

Chapter 35

"I can't believe it," said Bernard, astonished to hear how close Jefgeny Popov had come to becoming the third victim of Nurse Psychopath. "You read about these things, but you never imagine they happen in real life."

A sombre mood clouded Gwen's office as the medical team tried to process the information they now had. Graham had insisted they discuss it and debrief after he had been to see the captain.

"She might have killed me," Bernard continued.

"She wouldn't have tried it on any of us," said Graham.

Gwen, Bernard and Sarah looked at each other, acknowledging how close Bernard had come to being a victim.

"Don't you realise, Bernard? You were her alibi while she snooped around Jefgeny's room. I think she drugged you that night." Sarah saw the confused looks on Alex and Graham's faces and explained about the second morning of the cruise when Bernard had woken up to find Lauren in his bed.

Graham put a hand on Bernard's shoulder. "I'm sorry about your experience and glad you were drugged rather than killed. Why do you think she went back to the room?"

"Who knows – maybe she'd left something behind that might incriminate her, or perhaps she wanted to find Jefgeny and kill him," said Sarah.

"How did she carry on nursing?" asked Alex.

"People like her are renowned for being manipulative, and according to my friend in Connecticut, she was. She'd also been clever, offering to rotate around the hospital so no-one got to know her well, and subsequently suspicions weren't raised. It was only after a keen-eyed ward nurse in charge of supplies noticed insulin stocks didn't tally with those being administered that she got caught."

"So why didn't they realise then she might be killing patients?" asked Graham.

"She came up with a convincing story about visiting a slum where diabetic patients couldn't afford meds. They checked her story and confirmed that she did a lot of good in the slums. The hospital hierarchy gave her the opportunity to jump or be pushed. She chose to jump."

"So they believed she was some sort of misguided *Robin Hood*?" said Sarah. "Did she kill patients at the hospital?"

"That investigation's only just started, but I suspect if she's killed on this ship with such audacity, she's killed before."

"Why would she kill people in hospital, but not in a slum or Africa?"

"That we may never know," said Graham. "Perhaps her warped mind enjoyed playing God, choosing who should live and who should die. We're not certain she has killed before, and she might well have killed people in the slums, and in Africa too. I've called the doctor there and told him the bad news."

"What about the other hospitals she worked at?" asked Sarah.

"Fiction," answered Gwen. "I've had emails from all the hospitals listed on her CV – none of them have heard of her. The only places we're sure she worked at are the hospital in Connecticut, Future Motors and Africa. The local police are interviewing staff at Future Motors. I'm not sure whether we'll get any more information about that for now. She'll be handed over to the authorities when we arrive in New York, along with the man who attacked Rachel."

"What interesting cruises we enjoy when you and your friend are together, Sarah," said Graham. "I hope if there are any more shared cruises, the most exciting thing we encounter is who pays for drinks in the officers' mess."

They were brought back to reality when Sarah's radio burst into life with a call to a child suffering from sunburn. Letting out an exaggerated sigh, she stood up and grabbed the emergency case.

"Only one more sea day left – hurray!"

Day 6

Chapter 36

Sarah woke following the best night's sleep she'd had in ages. Her evening had been light, and pleased not to have encountered any real emergencies, she'd prayed for the first time in ages before going to bed, thanking God that Bernard had not been one of the victims of Lauren's killing spree.

The happiness transferred over to the morning; it was the final sea day before they were due to arrive in New York, and Sarah was looking forward to shore leave and shopping with Rachel. She ordered a room service breakfast and changed into her scrubs as she was only working the two surgeries today. Gwen was taking the on calls for the day as she would also be on shore leave tomorrow. With New York being an overnight stop, they were alternating leave, with half the team having one day off and the other half the second. After six days at sea, it was important they all stepped on land again.

Sarah pulled the case into the medical centre and wheeled it into Gwen's office before starting surgery. She finally got to run the blood tests on Jefgeny, and they revealed he was anaemic with abnormal liver function, pointing to early liver damage from excessive alcohol intake. She and Alex were going over the results as Eva was also anaemic.

"Eva just needs a bit of iron and some folic acid to help her through the pregnancy," said Alex. "She'll be fine with that. It's sad she will lose her job – it won't help her with an application for American citizenship." He shook his head.

Sarah felt sorry for Eva, whose only crime had been protecting the life of the man she loved. Now it seemed that unless he stopped drinking, his life wouldn't be that long anyway. They walked through to the infirmary to deliver the news to both patients, starting with Jefgeny.

"Now, Mr Popov, I have to tell you you're severely anaemic, and more than likely you have a stomach ulcer caused by drinking. On top of that, your liver is struggling to cope with your alcohol intake and you have the beginnings of liver cirrhosis." Alex allowed this information to sink in.

"Can you cure me?" Jefgeny asked, head down.

"We can give you medicine to heal the ulcer and you will need to have a tube passed into your stomach in hospital on land to find out how bad the damage is. If you're fired from the company, the cruise line insurance will no longer cover you."

Sarah's heart broke as she looked at the terror on Jefgeny's face. He'd already been through so much.

Alex continued. "In terms of the liver, that's down to you. If you want to see your child grow up, you need to stop drinking."

It sounded harsh, but Sarah knew Alex was trying his best to provoke Jefgeny to help himself. She wasn't sure whether the man could stop drinking if he lost his job, his insurance, and his girlfriend got deported.

Eva looked at him, pleading with him. "Jefgeny, please, for me and for our baby."

Jefgeny looked down and nodded. "I try."

Alex seized his opportunity. "I'll start you on stomach medication straight away and give you an eight-week supply. Miss Sipka won't be able to drink during pregnancy so that should help you. Do you have anywhere to go when you get to America – any family?"

Sarah knew the answer to this, but said nothing. As part of a witness protection programme, Jefgeny would have had to sever all links to his past. She wondered how he'd ended up on the cruise ship rather than being given funding to start a good new life. She'd hoped to ask him, but for now she needed to start surgery.

After surgery, the team ate lunch in the medical centre, courtesy of Raggie who brought the food up from the kitchen. Once lunch was over, they all dispersed. They discharged Jefgeny and Eva, with Eva returning to work and Jefgeny being under house arrest, confined to his room until the next day. Waverley had assigned a security guard to him.

Gwen, Bernard and Sarah were finishing up the last of the coffee when Gwen's computer beeped to announce an incoming email. She sashayed to the screen.

"You guys need to see this." She turned the screen towards them. It displayed a photo of Lauren entwined in the arms of a man. Sarah recognised the man.

"I need to find Rachel," she said as she ran from the office with Bernard in hot pursuit.

Chapter 37

Rachel was late, but saw Thomas at the front of the room, giving the group some last-minute instructions regarding the treasure hunt.

"Divide into groups, a minimum of two and a maximum of four. The sheets on the chairs contain the clues for the treasure hunt. We will let groups depart at ten minute intervals so we don't cause chaos around the ship. When the last group has gone, Rachel and I will follow to pick up any stragglers and help any of you who are struggling. Are we clear?"

"Clear," several people answered at once. Thomas beckoned to Rachel to take a seat, looking happier than he had the day before. Rachel watched the last group leave the room before speaking to him.

"Have you decided?" she asked.

"I have. I will go with you after this activity, on condition you join me on the treasure hunt," he teased.

"As you've already included me, I don't see how I can refuse. Anyway, it will be fun. It's years since I did a treasure hunt. We need to speak with the security chief straight after, though."

"I know." He put his head down before marching off. "Come on, then, time to go." Rachel followed him – it was easy for them because Thomas had set up the hunt with the aid of the cruise director and knew where to find all the clues.

It wasn't long before they found a group of three people wandering around on deck four. Thomas looked at the last clue they had found on their sheet before pointing them towards the guest services area.

"Aren't you going to let me find any clues?" asked Rachel, disappointed.

"Sorry, we don't have time. The groups will become impatient if I'm not around to help them when they get lost."

Forty-five minutes later, after helping numerous groups with their clues, Thomas led the way to the rear of the ship. Rachel followed him up multiple flights of steps until they were in a private area with artificial grass.

"Where's this, then? I've never been up here."

"It's a private party area, not in use today. It's one of the areas we hired for the tour group. The next party's tonight."

"Ooh, it's luxurious. Is there a clue up here?" Rachel looked around some false cordylines for clues.

"No, Rachel, I'm afraid not."

Something in his tone made her turn around. She saw the gun in his hand before anything else.

"Thomas, why are you holding a gun?"

"You know why, Rachel."

"Are you saying it was you all along? How did you get that gun on the ship?"

"It's one of the many things I own. It's undetectable to scanners and comes apart to go through X-rays. A prototype, but trust me, it's deadly."

"So what happens now? You shoot me and throw me overboard?" Her voice sounded calmer than she felt, and she was speaking loudly.

"That's about the sum of it. I'm sorry, I had no idea you were a cop when I invited you to tag along. It was my mistake, but your snooping has brought about the inevitable outcome."

Rachel decided the only thing to do was to play for time. With a dry mouth, she spoke.

"Well you could at least tell me what this is all about. What about the conversation between Asimov and Sergei?"

He laughed. "I had you fooled there, didn't I? They were arguing about how to surprise Lucretia for her birthday on the return journey. Asimov is going to propose, but they had different ideas about the menu. They played into my hands – these Russians get so excited, it was easy to convince you they were arguing about murder."

"So they had no part in the deaths of Nikolai or the crewman?"

"None." He smirked. "My sister is a nurse on board the ship and she's been doing some final calls."

He laughed, obviously not realising that Lauren had been arrested. Rachel didn't want to spook him by telling him.

"The man – Popov, as he's now called – was responsible for putting my father and my brother in jail. He and another man caused my father to kill himself because my mother returned to England in shame. Lauren and I vowed to get revenge on them. My sister likes killing people – she confided in me she killed patients in a hospital where she worked. I got her a job at a company we were stealing plans from to keep her out of trouble, but on this trip, I've let her do what she likes to do."

Rachel couldn't help but be disgusted at how lightly he dismissed murder. Thomas was in full boastful mode, almost wanting to tell her everything it seemed.

"I killed one traitor in Russia the day before the cruise, and now I will kill Popov, but first, I'll kill his girlfriend in front of him."

The conversation was taking a sinister turn. Rachel hoped to keep him calm, because if he got angry, he might just pull the trigger.

"What about Boris and the industrial espionage? I don't understand."

"Ah yes, Boris. All he's doing is smuggling copies of plans for a state of the art refrigeration system for a friend of

Asimov. Minor stuff, but hard to get hold of in Russia. I'm the one who will collect the blueprints for the new stealth aircraft. Everything I told you is true, but I'm the mastermind. I took over the business of export from my father and got a job as a cruise tour guide because it's the perfect vehicle for meeting up with buyers and sellers. This one is personal, though – unfinished business. Anyway, Rachel, I need to get back to the group, so I'm afraid your time is up."

"Did you cause the accident that put my friend's colleague's father in hospital?"

"Your friend?"

"My friend's also a nurse on the ship."

He looked shaky now, but recovered quickly. "Yes, Rachel. You need to understand, this is not personal; it's business – a multi-million dollar business. I like you, I do, and had I known you were a policewoman, I wouldn't have invited you along for the ride, but it's been a pleasure."

He lifted the gun, but a pair of strong arms grabbed him from behind, causing it to fall to the floor. Waverley held him in a vice-like grip and called for assistance. His security guards had been waiting in the wings and they now approached and cuffed Thomas.

"You took your time!" shouted Rachel.

"Don't worry – you were never in any danger. Look behind you." She turned and saw an officer with a rifle waving at her. "He would have shot if things had got out of hand."

"Out of hand – what do you call out of hand?"

"Sorry, we needed the confession." Waverley shrugged.

Thomas looked confused and angry.

"Thomas, I couldn't sleep last night. So many things didn't ring true – least of all, your translation of the Russian conversation. I speak very little Russian, but I do understand a few words, and 'birthday' and 'party' kept coming up in the conversation you were translating. And they never mentioned Nikolai. There were other things too. I suspected you were American. Even though you have mastered the English accent, you make mistakes, such as 'line' for queue and 'elevator' for a lift. On their own, they mean nothing, but last night, I put it all together and you became my prime suspect."

Thomas scowled. Waverley continued the story, looking chuffed.

"Miss Prince alerted me this morning, and we looked into you in great detail, Thomas Gabriel – or rather, Mr Timothy Blythe. We tracked down your mother, who hasn't heard from you in years. She says you are too much like your father."

"So what! You have no evidence I've done anything wrong. It's her word against mine. No court will convict me. I'll walk."

"Except that I'm wearing a wire – that's how they knew where we were." Rachel pulled up her outer blouse to reveal wires and a microphone. "Courtesy of the *Coral Queen*." She took the recording off and handed it to Waverley.

"I think you and your sister, who is already incarcerated in the ship's brig, will go away for a very long time, Mr Blythe. We will also hand over an important notebook I found in your safe to the FBI in the morning."

"How did you get in there?"

"Miss Prince has sharp eyes and watched you tap in the code and memorised it when she was with you yesterday. We copied it last night while you were busy with your guests. Mr Price will not be meeting up with you in New York as the police have already arrested him. There will not be much left of your little gang by the time Interpol has finished. You chose the wrong stooge, Mr Blythe.

"Rachel, Sarah's waiting for you in the main atrium – she almost gave the game away."

It was time to leave. "Goodbye, Thomas – or Timothy. I don't suppose we'll be meeting again. Nothing personal, of course!" She held her head up high and bounced down the steps, leaving Waverley and his officers to deal with Timothy Blythe.

Chapter 38

Sarah ran over as soon as Rachel arrived in the main atrium and hugged her tight. "Oh, Rachel – I was so worried about you. Waverley assured me you had it all under control when I tried to put out a ship-wide alert for you."

"What made you do that?"

"Gwen got a picture through today. It was a newspaper cutting about an industrial espionage gang leader who killed himself. The photo showed Lauren and her brother, Timothy Blythe, at the man's funeral, embracing, and I recognised him as your tour guide friend."

"Yes, it seems Timothy Blythe became Thomas Gabriel courtesy of deed poll to hide his past, but continue with his father's business."

"I was going to warn you, but Waverley said you'd worked it all out and would get a confession out of him. It has worried me sick something would go wrong – there's no way I could have done it."

"And I couldn't do what you do, so we'll just have to keep doing our own jobs."

"Except Waverley will offer you a security officer's job again, I'm sure."

"He already did – last night."

"And?"

"I'd rather go shopping in New York tomorrow, if you're still up for it?" Rachel laughed.

"Absolutely," replied Sarah.

"One thing, though – the ship's brig will be overcrowded tonight!"

"That's Waverley's problem. Lunch?" asked Sarah.

"Definitely, I'm starving."

Rachel was called into a meeting in Waverley's office that afternoon. It surprised her to see Asimov and Boris sitting down when she arrived.

"Ah, Miss Prince has arrived so we can start." Waverley showed Rachel to a seat.

"I demand to know what this is all about," Asimov barked.

"Me too," echoed Boris.

Me three! thought Rachel, but kept her thoughts to herself.

"Of course, gentlemen. First, I regret to inform you your tour guide, Thomas Gabriel, has been arrested on suspicion of murder and conspiracy to commit industrial espionage."

Rachel couldn't help smiling at Asimov's open mouth as he stared in disbelief.

Waverley was in his element. "I have spoken with Ronson Tours and another guide named Jeremiah Radley will join the ship tomorrow and take over Mr Gabriel's appointments."

"Well that's settled, then," said Asimov, shifting in his seat as if to leave.

"Not quite, sir. I must insist that you indulge me in a theory before you leave."

The men looked impatient, but Rachel guessed what might be coming.

"If it were to come to my attention, that someone might commit a crime in New York involving the handover of certain sensitive information regarding refrigeration equipment, I would have to move swiftly and inform the authorities. These theoretical people have committed no such crime at present, but I would value your opinion, gentlemen, whether you think such a crime might occur."

Asimov reddened, but then smiled. "I believe no such crime will happen. What do you think, Boris?"

"I don't believe anyone will commit such a crime, Mr Asimov." Boris looked relieved, almost joyful.

"Excellent," replied Waverley. "As a precaution, I must insist that diplomatic bags remain on board the ship while we are in port. I apologise in advance for the inconvenience. However, following the murder of one of your group, we need to ensure your safety by making thorough searches of people who return from shore leave."

"Chief, I understand," said Asimov. Rachel admired the man's ability to admit and accept defeat. "I'm due to dress for dinner now, so if you will excuse me."

He rose from his chair and left the room. Boris also got up to leave.

"Just one moment, Mr Stanislav. I wanted to let you know your brother in law is safe aboard ship and willing to meet up with you in secret later this evening – here are the arrangements." Waverley handed Boris an envelope.

"I would be very pleased to accept, as long as it does not put him in danger. My wife, his sister, misses him terribly."

"I guarantee his safety," said Waverley.

Boris pocketed the envelope and left the office, smiling. Rachel couldn't help smiling too.

"Thank you for that – I was pleased to be here."

"We're not finished yet." He picked up the phone. "Send them in." Rachel looked towards the door and saw Jefgeny and Eva escorted into the office. "Please take a seat," instructed Waverley.

They sat down, holding hands, preparing for the worst.

"Mr Popov, Miss Sipka, the captain has asked me to convey his disappointment with some of your actions during this cruise."

"Sorry, sir," said Jefgeny.

"However, he has spoken with the cruise line and explained the circumstances of what has happened, and we have both spoken to your senior officers. They agree that you should both keep your jobs, if you would like them, on condition that no such thing happens again, and that you, Mr Popov, work with Dr Romano to overcome your health issues."

Jefgeny and Eva hugged each other. "Thank you so much, we will do everything you say."

"The United States of America owes you a debt of gratitude, Mr Popov. Dr Romano has arranged for you to have an endoscopy at 10am tomorrow at Queen Cruises' expense as you remain covered as an employee. Now I suggest that you both get back to work."

They beamed as they left. "Yes, sir."

Rachel was over the moon. "I can't wait to tell Sarah, she'll be ecstatic. She was so worried about Jefgeny."

"I love my job sometimes," said Waverley. "Enjoy the rest of the cruise, Rachel. I hope you will stay out of trouble for the remaining eight days, if that's at all possible."

"Oh, it's possible," Rachel said as she floated out the door.

THE

Author's Note

Thank you

If you have enjoyed reading this book, please leave an honest review on Amazon and/or any other platform you may use. I love receiving feedback from readers and can assure you that I read every review. Keep an eye out for book 3 in the Rachel Prince Mystery series. *Killer Cruise* is due for release in spring 2019.

Keep in Touch:

Website: www.dawnbrookespublishing.com.
Facebook: https://www.facebook.com/dawnbrookespublishing/
Twitter: @dawnbrookes1

About the Author

Dawn Brookes is a fun-loving and light hearted person, with a creative side that comes across in her writing.

The surname of her protagonist comes in honour of her childhood dog, a boxer called *Prince*, who used to put his head on her knee while she lost herself in books.

Author of bestselling eBook *Hurry up Nurse: memoirs of nurse training in the 1970s* and *Hurry up Nurse 2: London calling*, Dawn worked in a career spanning thirty-nine years.

Dawn grew up in Leicester, later moved to London and Berkshire and now lives in Derby.

Acknowledgements

Thank you to my editor Alison Jack for her kind comments about the book and for suggestions, corrections and amendments that make it a better read.

Thanks to my early beta readers for comments, suggestions and for their time.

Thanks to my immediate circle of friends who are so patient with me when I'm absorbed by my fictional world and for your continued support in all my endeavours.

I have to say thank you to my sea loving friends for joining me on some of the most precious experiences of my life and to the cruise lines for making every holiday a special one.

Other Books by Dawn Brookes

Rachel Prince Mysteries
A Cruise to Murder

Memoirs
Hurry up Nurse: memoirs of nurse training in the 1970s
Hurry up Nurse 2: London calling

Coming Soon 2019
Book 3 in the Rachel Prince Mystery Series, Killer Cruise

Book 4 in the Rachel Prince Mystery Series, Dying to Cruise

Book 6 in the Rachel Prince Mystery Series, Christmas Cruise Caper

Book 3 in the Hurry up Nurse series, Hurry up Nurse 3

Printed in Poland
by Amazon Fulfillment
Poland Sp. z o.o., Wrocław

49293294R00277